W9-BTO-584

The Black Stallion Returns

What was the motive of the night prowler in attempting to destroy the Black, one of the world's most famous horses? The prowler left behind him a gold medallion on which was embossed the figure of a large white bird, its wings outstretched in flight. Was it the Phoenix, that fabulous bird of mythology which symbolized the resurrection of the dead? If so, what did it signify? Where would it lead Alec Ramsay, young owner of the Black?

This is the story of a boy's great love for his horse. A love that led him halfway around the world—across the vast white sands of Rub' al Khali, the Great Central Desert of Arabia—to intrigue and adventure such as few have ever known.

Books by
WALTER FARLEY

The Black Stallion
The Black Stallion Returns
Son of the Black Stallion
The Island Stallion
The Black Stallion and Satan
The Black Stallion's Blood Bay Colt
The Island Stallion's Fury
The Black Stallion's Filly
The Black Stallion Revolts
The Black Stallion's Sulky Colt
The Island Stallion Races
The Black Stallion's Courage
The Black Stallion Mystery
The Black Stallion and Flame
The Black Stallion Challenged!
The Black Stallion's Ghost
The Black Stallion and the Girl
The Horse-Tamer
Man o' War

*All titles available in both paperback
and hardcover editions*

The Black Stallion Returns

By WALTER FARLEY

Random House New York

Copyright, 1945, by Walter Farley
Copyright renewed 1973 by Walter Farley
Printed in the United States of America
Published simultaneously in Canada by
Random House of Canada Ltd.

Library of Congress Cataloging in Publication Data

Farley, Walter
  The black stallion returns, by Walter Farley.
  New York, Random house [1945]
  Sequel to the author's Black stallion.
1. Horses—Legends and stories.   I. Title
PZ10.3.F22Bm   45–8763
Library of Congress   [64j4]
ISBN: 0–394–80602–6 (trade hardcover)
        0–394–90602–0 (library binding)
        0–394–83610–3 (trade paperback)

*To Rosemary and the boys and girls
who asked for this sequel*

Contents

Night Attack

1

Night hung black and heavy about the old barn. An iron gate creaked a short distance away and a few minutes later the short figure of a man slid alongside the barn. As he moved cautiously forward his fat, gloved hand felt the wood. The man stopped as he neared the door and his hand dug into his right coat pocket. Fumbling, he searched for something. Not finding it, he uttered an oath and reached awkwardly across to his left-hand pocket. He pulled the empty sleeve from the pocket and reached inside, withdrawing a long hypodermic needle. His dark-skinned face creased into folds of fatty tissue as he smiled. Moving forward once again, he did not bother to replace the empty coat sleeve and it hung limply at his side in the still air.

The prowler reached the door. Carefully he opened it and slid inside. His eyes, already accustomed to the darkness, made out the stalls on the other side of the barn. As he moved toward them, his thumb slipped to the back of the hypodermic needle.

The hard ring of a horse's hoofs against the floor came from one of the stalls. Then a long and slender neck that arched to a small, savagely beautiful head peered over the door. Thin-skinned nostrils quivered as black ears pitched forward. The prowler, halfway to the stall door, had stopped. The horse shook his long black mane and a powerful foreleg struck the door.

A board creaked as the man moved closer. Baring his teeth, the horse whistled the shrill, loud scream of a wild stallion. As the whistle resounded through the barn, the prowler moved forward. He would have to work fast. Mincing steps carried his round body to the stall door with amazing speed. He opened it, but fell back as the black stallion struck at him.

Gripping the hypodermic firmly, the prowler advanced again, more cautiously this time. He stopped and his fat face twitched nervously. The giant horse rose on his hind legs, mouth open and teeth bared. As he came down, the man lunged at him, but the horse's foreleg caught him in the groin. The attacker turned gray beneath his bronze skin. Staggering back, he attempted to close the stall door behind him. The stallion, halfway through the door, rose again on his hind legs as the man stumbled and fell to the floor. Thrashing hoofs pawed the air above him. The hypodermic dropped from his hand as the giant form began to descend. The man rolled fast, avoiding the stallion's hoofs by inches. Climbing to his feet, he ran frantically for the barn door.

Outside, he heard voices coming from the direction of the gate and, turning, stumbled off into the night, the empty coat sleeve waving slightly at his side.

A few minutes later a young boy, carrying a flashlight, ran up to the barn door. Following him was a bowlegged man who moved with jerky strides.

"Something must be wrong, Henry," the youth shouted. "The door's open!"

Henry grabbed the flashlight. "Yeah, I'll go in, Alec. Y'stay here, just in case . . ."

Impatiently, Alec waited while Henry entered the barn. A hand swept nervously across his pug nose as he pinched his nostrils. There was a worried expression on his freckled face. If anything had happened to the Black! Then he heard the short neigh and the sound of the stallion's hoofs against the floor. His tense body relaxed. Everything was probably all right. Looking around the yard, his gaze swept to the open field. It was getting light and already he could make out the high white fence at the north end. There was no one around. He tightened the belt holding up his corduroys and then pushed a hand through his red, tousled hair.

Turning on the lights, Henry appeared in the doorway. He beckoned Alec inside.

The Black was in his stall. He whistled softly when he saw Alec and shook his black mane, which mounted high, then fell low, like a crest.

"Find anything, Henry?"

"He was out of his stall. Someone's been here . . . there's been a fight of some kind. He's sweated." Henry ran a gnarled hand over the stallion's body as it glistened in the bright light.

The Black moved nervously around his stall and didn't quiet until Alec's hand rested on the thin-skinned nostrils. "He seems to be okay though, Henry."

"Yep." Henry was quiet. In his hand he studied a long glass object wrapped in his handkerchief.

"What is it?" Alec asked.

"A hypo."

"You mean a hypodermic needle?" Alec asked incredulously. "You found it here?"

"Yep . . . on the floor."

"What's it mean, Henry?" Alec moved away from the Black to get a closer view of the glass tube.

"Looks as if someone intended to use it on the Black."

"Y'mean" . . . Alec's heart thumped hard. "Henry, are you *sure* it hasn't been used?"

"It's filled. We'll get the stuff analyzed today by the police and find out what it is. Maybe it'll give us a clue of some kind." He wrapped the needle in the handkerchief and said, "Also, there might be some fingerprints. . . ."

Alec moved over to the Black again. The stallion lowered his head and, rubbing it, Alec asked, "But why would anyone want to harm him, Henry?"

"Your guess is as good as mine, Alec." Then Henry added, ". . . perhaps better."

"What do you mean?"

Henry moved over to Alec and placed a long arm on the stall door. "Well, here's how I figure it out. The Black is a valuable horse since he beat out Sun Raider and Cyclone last June. There's no doubt that he's the fastest thing to set foot on any track here or abroad. Now to my way of thinkin' there's a good many reasons why somebody would want to steal the Black. He couldn't be raced but he could be used for stud . . . that horse could do much to improve the blood line of the American thoroughbred. . . ."

"But, Henry," Alec interrupted, "he isn't a registered thoroughbred. There are no papers . . . we know so little about where he came from or anything. If they won't let us race him any more because no one knows who his sire and dam were, I don't see how anyone could use him for stud either and get away with it."

"Some folks might be able to get around it," Henry answered. "But let me finish. Now whether or not anyone could get around the lack of registration papers for the Black is beside the point. Nobody tried to steal the Black . . . they tried to kill him; or at least that's what I think we'll find when we've had this stuff analyzed." His gaze shifted to the hypodermic needle, then back to Alec. "Why would anyone want to kill the Black?"

"Hey, Henry, I don't see how anyone could be that cruel. . . .Then a vivid picture flashed before Alec; that of the small Arabian port where they had docked on his way home from visiting Uncle Ralph in India and where he had first seen the Black. Again he was looking down from the deck of the old freighter, *Drake,* and beholding a sight that made his body tremble with anger: The glistening black horse, too big to be pure Arabian, high on his hind legs; forelegs striking furiously in the air; white lather running from his body. And around his savage head was tied a scarf, covering his eyes. Two ropes led from the halter and four natives were attempting to pull him toward the ship. Standing behind the stallion was a dark-skinned man wearing a white turban. In his hand he held a hard whip, which he raised menacingly. Then he let the whip fall on the Black's hindquarters and the stallion screamed. It was unlike anything Alec had ever heard before; it rose to a high-pitched whistle, the cry of a wild, unbroken stallion! He bolted, and if Alec had ever seen hate expressed by a horse, he had seen it then. The stallion struck one of the men holding the rope; he went down and lay in a still, lifeless heap. Eventually they had gotten the giant horse on the ship and in his stall.

Alec looked at Henry and realized the old man knew what he had been thinking. "You believe it might have been the man on the boat? Is that what you mean, Henry?"

"Could be, Alec."

"But the storm, shipwreck . . . he was drowned. I saw him go down with my own eyes."

"And his name wasn't listed among the survivors?" Henry asked.

"No . . . there were only a few, as you know."

"The last you saw of him was when he fell overboard . . . that right, Alec?"

"He didn't exactly fall, Henry. He jumped for an already filled lifeboat and missed . . . he didn't have a life jacket and there was such a sea that I couldn't see him after that. A few minutes later the *Drake* cracked up and I was in the water, too. I saw the Black and the rope on his halter and grabbed it. The next thing I knew I was on the island. You know the rest. . . ."

"And after they found you . . . and during your trip

home . . . you heard nothin' to indicate that the Black's owner was alive?"

"No, Henry . . . nothing. One lifeboat containing ten people was found, that's all, and he wasn't among them. I'm sure he couldn't have lived in that heavy sea. Another thing, Henry, I don't think for a moment that he was the owner of the Black."

"Y'mean you think he had stolen him?"

"Yes. For one thing, he acted as though he had . . . always kept to himself. Then he was too cruel to the Black. If he owned him, he wouldn't have done the things that he did."

"Can't tell, Alec. I've seen some purty hard horse owners in my time. Still, maybe you're right . . . he's a lot of horse and even without seein' him run some people would pay a mighty handsome price for him."

As Henry walked across the room, his foot struck a small metallic object. He stooped and picked it up. "What's this?"

"Looks like a gold neck chain . . . but what's that disc in the center, Henry?"

Henry walked over underneath the light and took a closer look at the disc. "Seems to be a bird of some kind," he muttered. He handed the chain to Alec. "Make it out?" he asked.

A large bird carved in white ivory was embossed upon a gold disc which hung from the chain. Its long, powerful wings were outstretched in flight. Alec noticed the beak, hooked at the point, and long claws on short, strong legs. Two tiny red stones had been used for eyes. "I'm sure it's a falcon, Henry. My Uncle Ralph had a couple when I was in India and I've seen others . . . although never any white ones like this. They're usually a dusky color."

Henry was silent for a few minutes. He took the chain from Alec and rolled it in his hands. "Cinch that this wasn't made in the States, Alec," he said.

"Guess not . . . the work is too fine. Henry, this may mean . . ."

". . . that I may be right. That the guy on the ship is still alive and wants to kill the Black for some reason."

"Or, Henry, that someone else from Arabia or somewhere in the Middle East wants to kill him."

"Yeah." Henry walked over to the Black and placed a hand on the flaring nose.

The sun had risen well above the trees at the east end of the field when Alec left the barn and headed for the gate and home. His feet dragged along the graveled driveway. He hadn't wanted to leave, but Henry had talked him into it, knowing that this was the week before final exams. Exams! School! What did they matter now! Someone had attempted to kill the Black, his horse. And whoever it was might return to try again.

Henry had assured him that he would guard the stallion until Alec returned later in the day. The police would be notified, for he would stop in at the station on his way to school. Alec was sure his father would see to it that a policeman stayed near the barn at night, and Alec had every intention of sleeping in the barn with the Black. They'd change the locks on the iron gate and barn door. Summer vacation would follow next week's exams, then he'd spend the next three months, night and day, with his horse.

He reached the high iron gate. The lock wasn't broken and Alec doubted that anyone had scaled the fence with all that barbed wire running around the top. Obviously, the intruder had had a key or picked the lock. Still, perhaps Tony had left it open when he and old Napoleon, his gray, sway-backed horse, who shared the barn with the Black, had gone to the market to load the wagon with vegetables for the day's business. There was a good chance, too, that the prowler, knowing what time Tony left each morning, had slipped inside after Tony had driven Napoleon through the gate without his being aware of it. He'd have to speak to Tony tonight.

Alec closed the gate behind him, locked it, and headed for the large brown house across the street. He walked slowly in spite of the fact that he knew it was getting late and he'd have to hurry if he was going to stop in at the police station and still make his first class.

Someone cruel and vicious wanted to put an end to the Black. Why? What motive could he possibly have? True, Alec knew little of the stallion's past. Perhaps, as Henry had suggested, the answer lay there . . . somewhere in Arabia.

Abu Já Kub ben Ishak

2

Later that afternoon Alec hurried home from school. He had cut his last class and was anxious to find out what Henry had learned from the police. The content of the hypodermic needle . . . was it poisonous? And the fingerprints . . . would they furnish a clue to the identity of the Black's attacker? The police had listened to his story at the station and before Alec left the captain had ordered a patrol car to go to the barn.

As Alec approached his home he saw a black limousine parked in front; behind it was a police car. He broke into a run, and nearing the house saw the plump figure of his mother standing on the porch. "Mom," Alec shouted, "what's happened? The police . . . they're still here?"

His mother's voice was unemotional, but Alec noted that her face was taut and tired-looking. "They returned a short while ago,'' she said. ''A man's with them, who claims to own the Black.'' She paused, then added softly, ''Better go over to the stable, Alec.''

Alec turned and without a word ran toward the gate, his legs pounding furiously on the pavement. Reaching the gate, he flung it open. Blood ran from his lower lip, which was held tightly between clenched teeth. A hundred thoughts rushed through his brain. This, on top of what happened last night! Somebody claiming the Black as his! Perhaps this was the man who had attempted to kill the Black and, having failed, was attempting to get him this way! Alec pulled up in front of the door to the barn. Inside he saw Henry talking to a tall, elderly man. Behind them stood two policemen.

Henry was the first to see Alec's white face. ''Alec,'' he said, ''this is Mr. Abu . . .'' He stopped and turned to the man beside him.

''Abu Já Kub ben Ishak,'' the stranger finished.

Alec's eyes swept to the Black safely in his stall, then back to the stranger. His skin was the color of old mahogany and was tough and dry. He was tall and slight with sparkling black eyes. A white beard, cut to a point, jutted out when he talked; his hair was steel gray. Alec found it difficult to guess his age. He wore a brown coat of English cloth and an embroidered waistcoat.

''Mr. Ishak owns the Black, Alec.''

It was Henry's voice, low and strained. Alec turned and faced his friend; there was a tightening in his throat. He swallowed; then the heat of anger rushed through his body. ''But, Henry . . .'' he almost shouted. ''How do we know? Last night . . . the hypodermic . . . the gold chain. Has this nothing to do with it?'' His gaze swept to the policeman, then back to Henry again. "Were the contents of the hypodermic poisonous? Were there any fingerprints? Isn't it strange that this man should turn up now . . . after last night?"

They were silent when Alec finished, then Henry said, "Yes, Alec, it's strange and all pretty hard to believe . . . especially comin' all at once like this." He paused, then continued. "This morning when the police came they took the hypo and gold chain back to the station. Later on they came back and told me the stuff in the hypo was a deadly poison. No fingerprints were found. An hour ago they showed up again, bringin' Mr. Ishak here with 'em. He had papers which proved he owned the Black."

"I'd like to see them," Alec interrupted, turning to Abu Já Kub ben Ishak.

The tall man handed the papers to Alec, who read them carefully. After a moment he looked at the police-men. One of them, guessing what was foremost in his mind, said, "We've checked Washington and he's who he says he is. When he showed up at the station this afternoon we were suspicious, too."

Abu Já Kub ben Ishak looked at Alec and his face was grave. "Perhaps," he said, "it is best that I explain why I went to the station." He paused, and his voice softened. "It was simply to identify myself, for I knew that it would be necessary before I could claim my horse. You see, he had been stolen from me. It wasn't until reports reached me in Arabia of a great black stallion beating Sun Raider and Cyclone that I guessed the Black might possibly be my horse, Shêtân. I went to the American consulate and in time learned the story of how you and the stallion had survived the sinking of the *Drake*. Then there were the news pictures and I was certain that it was Shêtân.''

Alec looked into the serious black eyes of the Arab. ''If all you say is true,'' he asked, ''how do you account for the attack on the Black last night?''

Abu Já Kub ben Ishak was silent.

Henry said, ''We thought the guy who stole the Black might still be alive. Would he have any reason for killin' him?''

The Arab's face was like stone. He took the hypodermic from Henry's hand and examined it.

Watching him, Alec said, ''Then there was a gold chain left behind. Show it to him, Henry.''

Henry held the chain out to Abu Já Kub ben Ishak. There was no change in the Arab's set face, no sign of recognition. Yet, Alec felt something in the still tenseness of the barn. He was certain that the great bird with outstretched wings was not unfamiliar to Abu Já Kub ben Ishak.

Finally, the Arab spoke and his voice was cold and brittle. ''It is not known to me,'' he said. Alec noticed that he did not ask to see the chain as he had the hypodermic. His whole attitude convinced Alec that there was much that he was keeping to himself. ''I'll return for Shêtân in an hour,'' he said curtly. Then he nodded to the policemen, and they left the barn with him.

Alec and Henry didn't speak, nor did they look at each other. Silently they walked to the stall door. The Black peered over, his eyes wild and staring. Abu Ishak was no stranger to him. He shifted his feet and flecked his long black tail; his nostrils were red and dilated.

Alec ran a hand through the stallion's heavy mane. "Fella, what are we going to do?" His voice was low and strained. Finally, he turned and met Henry's grave eyes. "Do you think he'd sell him, Henry?"

"No, Alec. He seems to want him pretty bad. And even if he would he'd ask a mighty high price for him. Where'd we get the money?"

"I'd get it . . . somewhere." Alec was quiet for a moment. The Black nuzzled his neck. "Henry! I've got it! Maybe Mr. Volence or Mr. Hurst, owners of Cyclone and Sun Raider, might help us. They could lend us the money!"

"Yeah, they might at that. They're both interested enough in him. Worth tryin' if Abu will sell."

The minutes passed. Henry walked awkwardly around the barn rearranging bridles and saddles that didn't need it. Finally he walked to the doorway and sat down on the step. Better to leave Alec alone with his horse, he didn't have much time. Henry drew out his pocket knife and began whittling a piece of wood. Funny, the way you could become attached to some horses. It was no new experience for him. There had been Dynamo, the tough little bay that had run away with him in his first workout. He'd just been an exercise boy then—a kid, like Alec. Suppose he would have been fired, too, if Dynamo hadn't run the fastest quarter mile ever seen on the old Empire track. Yes, they were all good memories. There had been a few others in the years that followed . . . Chang, who could outsprint the sprinters and outstay the stayers; Me Too, who used to stand as quiet as a pony at the barrier waiting patiently for the race to begin while all the others fought to break out of line, yet was never beaten. Those two were good horses that he'd never forget.

Then, years after he'd retired and the missus had done all she could to make him forget the track, along had come the Black and Alec, in spite of her. The black stallion was a better horse than he'd ever ridden or trained. Guess he knew that the first night he'd seen him. He had to laugh when he remembered how Alec, the kid from across the street, had talked the missus into letting him keep his horse in their barn. "His horse" . . . she'd probably visioned some old swayback like Napoleon. Funny, she never rebelled when she found out. Perhaps, Henry mused, there's more horse in her than she lets on. Or maybe it was because, like everybody else, she felt sorry for Alec after all he'd gone through. He'd read about the *Drake* going down off the coast of Spain and had been told that Alec was one of the passengers, coming back from India after spending his summer vacation with his uncle.

He'd never paid much attention to Alec. Saw him coming and going to school, but that was about all . . . a skinny kid, who gave the impression to anyone who didn't know him that he was pretty much the studious type. When the report had come through that there were no survivors, he'd gone to see Mr. and Mrs. Ramsay. They had been pretty broken up, but they hadn't given up hope that Alec was still alive. "He's a strong youngster," Mr. Ramsay had said.

Five months later Alec had returned, and not alone. With him was the Black, unbroken and untamed. Yes, and unapproachable to all but Alec. Between him and the black stallion had grown a friendship that Henry in all his years around men and horses had never seen equalled. The Black was wild and a killer, no doubt about that . . . even now.

Henry smiled a bit as he remembered the time they'd had breaking the stallion to bridle and saddle. Then a little later had come the night training sessions at the track. Finally, the big race . . . and long would racing fans remember and talk about how he'd drubbed Sun Raider and Cyclone, the two fastest horses in America. Perhaps never again would they see a horse like the Black.

Nor would they see the Black.

Henry glanced at his watch. Pretty near an hour since Abu Ishak had left. A few minutes later he closed his knife as he saw a horse van coming down the street. He rose slowly to his feet and entered the barn.

"They're comin', Alec," he said. The boy's back was toward him, his face hard against the stallion's neck.

"He saved my life, Henry," Alec said. He attempted to go on, but his voice broke. His shoulders swept forward and Henry knew that he was crying.

"Yeah, I know, Alec . . ." Henry stopped and turned back toward the door.

The van was at the gate now and soon would be at the door. Henry walked over to Alec and his long arm descended on the boy's shoulder. The stallion tossed his head, baring his teeth. "Look, kid . . . I could tell you about horses that I've loved and lost in my time, but it wouldn't do any good. Guess there's no love greater than yours for the Black, 'cept maybe his for you. I'm not goin' to tell you that you'll forget him, either, 'cause you won't. But cryin's not going to help. You're a gutty kid or you wouldn't be here today, so pull yourself together and let's try to figure somethin' out between the two of us.''

Alec's hands swept across his eyes, then he turned to Henry. "Sure, Henry. . . .''

"We're up against a pretty high stone wall, Alec. By law and every right, the Black belongs to Abu Ishak. If he'll sell him, we'll get the money some place. If he won't, the Lord only knows what we can do. I'll talk to him and tell him what's grown up between you and the Black and hope he understands. Puttin' our cards on the table, we know that he's traveled halfway around the world for the Black. You don't do that unless you want somethin' pretty bad and have a mighty good reason for wantin' him that bad. He doesn't seem like an unreasonable guy, though, so maybe he'll listen and understand.''

"You don't think, Henry, that he had anything to do . . . with last night?"

"No. Abu Ishak wants his horse alive. Somebody else wants him done away with. Who it might be, I don't know. Maybe he knows, but he isn't tellin'. The medallion didn't mean anything to him, at any rate.''

"I think it did, Henry . . . for some reason I can't explain.''

The van had stopped in front of the barn. Henry walked to the door, followed by Alec.

Abu Ishak and a policeman were coming up the driveway. "I'll talk to him now. You stay here,'' Henry told Alec.

The stallion neighed and Alec went to him.

Ten minutes later the Arab entered the barn with Henry close behind. Alec's eyes swept to Henry's face and saw what he'd hoped he wouldn't see.

"He won't sell, Alec." It was Henry's voice. Alec looked at Abu Ishak.

"You won't, sir . . . not for any price?" he asked.

The Arab's eyes met Alec's. They seemed kind and Alec waited hopefully. "Mr. Dailey has told me how much my horse means to you. But, my son, an Arab's horse is not for sale; our horses are part of ourselves. At home we have our families, but in the desert our horses are our only company, and men do not sell their friends." He paused, withdrawing a wallet from his inside coat pocket. "I'd like to repay you for all you have done. Will you take this?"

Alec shook his head. "No, thanks, sir," he replied quietly.

Abu Já Kub ben Ishak looked at Henry. They both knew that it was useless to attempt to alter Alec's decision.

The driver of the van, who had been standing just inside the door, moved toward the stall. In his hand he held a lead rope. Abu Ishak stopped him. "I'll take him," he said.

Alec and Henry watched as Abu approached the stall. He moved quietly and without hesitation. Reaching the door, he opened it. The stallion's body trembled but he didn't strike, nor were his teeth bared. If Alec had any doubts about Abu's being the owner of the Black, they were gone, for no one, with the exception of Henry and himself, had ever approached the stallion without being

struck at by hoofs that moved with the speed of a
striking cobra.

Abu Ishak walked up to the stallion, unafraid. He
placed a hand gently upon the Black's glistening neck.
He spoke to him softly in Arabic and the stallion's ears
pricked forward. Swiftly Abu Ishak fastened the lead
rope to the halter. He ran his hands down the stallion's
legs; then, taking a step backward, he stood staring at
him. Many men had looked at the Black, but Alec had
never seen one look like this. Finally, he turned to
them. "You have been good to Shêtân," he said slowly.
"He has developed into a very fine horse." He lowered
his voice until Alec and Henry could barely make out his
words. "It is possible that time has not been wasted."

The Black half-reared when Abu Ishak began to lead
him from the stall, and for a moment Alec thought he
was going to strike. The Arab stood motionless, although
his eyes followed the stallion's ascent. The Black descended and stood still; his head turned in Alec's
direction and he whistled softly.

Alec stood still, he couldn't move. His horse . . .
would life be worth living without him? He held out his
hand. "Hey, Black". . . the words formed in his throat
but he could not get them out. The stallion was through
the stall door, Abu Ishak beside him. His hoofs rang on
the floor as he moved toward Alec. Reaching him, he
lowered his small head, the black mane falling down
over his bewildered eyes. Alec mechanically pushed it
away and rubbed his forehead, as he'd always done.
Suddenly he realized that this was the last time he'd
hold his horse and his arms fell around the long neck as

he pressed his head hard against the stallion's forehead.

Minutes passed and it was quiet in the barn. Then Alec looked up and his gaze met Abu Ishak's. "You'll be good to him?"

Abu Ishak nodded.

Alec's hand slipped from the Black's forehead to the mane. Walking slowly, he passed his horse, his fingers trailing along the black coat; then he went to the small tack room in the back of the barn. There he sat on a trunk, knees and fingers pressed together over the bridge of his nose. He tried not to hear the sound of the Black's hoofs as he left the barn, the shrill whistle. Then came the roar of the van's engine, the grinding of gears, and the hard rubber wheels on the gravel driveway.

His horse was gone. Would he ever see him again?

Bloodlines

3

Alec's father allowed the evening newspaper to fall to his lap and withdrew his long legs from the footstool in front of him. Through the porch screens he could see the sun setting behind Dailey's barn. He turned to his wife, who sat sewing beside him. "Gettin' dark, Belle. You'll hurt your eyes."

She laid Alec's corduroy pants down on her lap and removed her glasses. "Just patching up his riding pants again. He might want them, you know."

"Yes, he might. Hope so." Mr. Ramsay rose to his feet. "Know where he went, Belle?"

"He said he was going for a walk." Mrs. Ramsay picked up her sewing again. "I'm worried about him, Bill. He hasn't eaten much . . . nothing appeals to him."

"Glad he's out of his room, anyway. He's done

nothing but coop himself up there for the last two weeks.''

''But he's been studying hard, Bill. And he did so well in his final exams.'' Then she added proudly, ''One of his friends told me today that Alec got the highest marks in his graduating class.''

''Yes, it's great, Belle. But it's still not like Alec to study hard. Of course, we both know the reason was that he wanted to take his mind off the Black. Wonder what he'll do now, though, with school over for the summer?''

Mrs. Ramsay looked up from her sewing. ''Do you think we could afford to get him a horse to replace the Black? It could be his graduation present.''

''Guess we could afford it all right, Belle. Don't know as it'll do any good, though. No horse could ever replace the Black as far as Alec's concerned.'' Mr. Ramsay sat down in his chair again and put his legs back on the footstool. ''Might ask him tonight how he feels about getting another horse,'' he continued. ''After all there's a long summer ahead and in his present frame of mind he'll want to be kept busy.''

It was after dark when Alec returned. He greeted his parents and then sat down.

After a few minutes' silence, Mr. Ramsay said, ''You certainly did well in your exams, son. We're mighty proud of you.''

''Thanks, Dad.''

Alec's father filled his pipe, then lighted it carefully before he spoke again. ''Anything special you'd like as a graduation present, Alec?''

''No, Dad, thanks . . .''

"Your mother and I thought you might like a horse——" He stopped. He had been going to add "to take the place of the Black" but thought better of it.

Alec didn't answer for a minute, and when he did speak his voice was low, so low that it was hardly audible. "I don't think so, Dad . . . thanks . . . not now, anyway." He rose to his feet. "I think I'll go up to my room, if you don't mind, there's a book . . ." He walked quickly inside the house.

The following day Alec visited the old barn for the first time since the Black's departure. Nearing it, he heard Tony's voice. "That'sa good-a horse, Napoleon. Tomorrow you feel-a beeg again." Alec glanced at his watch. It was early in the afternoon for Tony and Napoleon to have completed their rounds.

When he entered the barn he saw Tony alone with Napoleon. The little Italian huckster had the old gray horse's head between his hands and was looking at him worriedly. "Anything the matter, Tony?" Alec asked after a moment's hesitation.

"'Allo, Aleec. It'sa da Nappy, he no feel so good."

Walking over to them, Alec ran his hand across the horse's back. "He's getting old, Tony. Have you seen a vet?"

"No. Napoleon, he no need a vet. He still wan young feller. Know what'sa da matta with him? He misses da big Black, that's all."

"Yeah, Tony . . . guess that's it. And I'm sure the Black misses him."

Tony led Napoleon into his stall, and Alec walked to the barn door. Outside he saw Henry. Calling, he ran toward him.

Henry smiled as Alec came up. "Missed you," he said, "but imagined exams were keepin' you pretty busy. How'd they go?"

"Okay," Alec said, "passed 'em all."

They walked to the barn and sat down on the bench. Finally, Tony came out. "'Allo, Henree," he said, "what'sa new?"

"Nothin', Tony. Same old stuff. Napoleon any better?"

"He's-a okay. Just what ya call it . . . depressed? Anyway, he miss-a da Black."

"He'll be all right in a few days," Henry assured him.

"You betch. Time-a heals everythin'." His black eyes shifted to Alec. "Well-a hafta go home to da wife and bambinos. Addio!"

A few minutes after Tony had left, Alec and Henry saw a limousine pull up in front of the gate. A tall man got out, pushed his hat to the back of his head, and looked inquiringly in the direction of the barn.

"Say, Henry!" Alec shouted. "That looks a lot like Mr. Volence!"

"Bejabers! It sure does. C'mon."

The two ran toward the gate. Neither had seen the wealthy owner of Sun Raider since the big race in Chicago, when the Black had beaten his horse.

Alec was the first to recognize him. "It's Mr. Volence all right, Henry," he shouted.

"Yeah. Wonder what he wants?"

Mr. Volence met them at the gate. "Henry! Alec! It's good seeing you again!" His large, heavily jowled face creased in a big grin.

A few minutes later they walked toward the barn. "So

this is where you keep that black devil," Mr. Volence said. "Tell me, has he calmed down any or is he as wild as ever?"

Henry looked at Alec. Alec shoved his hands in his pockets and said quietly, "He doesn't live here any more, Mr. Volence."

"You . . . you mean you sold him?"

"No," Alec explained. "His real owner turned up."

Then Alec told him the whole story. When he had finished, Mr. Volence walked slowly over to the bench and sat down. "That's like something out of a book," he said. "You know," he continued, "one of the reasons I came to New York was to see if you wouldn't sell the Black. I've retired Sun Raider to stud at my farm in Kentucky, but I still need a few more good stallions. The Black could have done much to improve the blood line of the American thoroughbred, you know. At least, that's my belief."

"That's just what I said," Henry agreed.

Alec looked at Mr. Volence. "There's still more to the story . . . something that happened the night before Abu Ishak showed up." Then he proceeded to tell him about the mysterious night visitor who had attempted to kill the Black.

"Whew!" Mr. Volence said, when Alec finished. "And you don't think there's any connection between Abu Ishak and the Black's attacker?"

Alec's gaze shifted to Henry, then back to Mr. Volence. "There may be a connection somewhere," he said. "I'm sure he recognized the medallion on the gold chain."

"He may have recognized it, Alec," Henry insisted,

"but I'm certain he didn't have anything to do with the attack on the Black."

Mr. Volence nodded. "I'm inclined to agree with Henry, Alec. Abu Ishak would have no reason for wanting to harm his own horse."

"You're probably right," Alec said, "but still . . ."

The three sat in silence for a few minutes. Finally, Mr. Volence slapped his hands on his knees and said, "Well, I guess it'll be one of those unsolved mysteries. Too bad the Black got away. We'll probably never see another like him." He stood up. "I plan to go abroad in a few weeks to see if I can't pick up some stallions."

Alec eyed Mr. Volence. "Where do you think you'll go, sir?" he asked. Henry noted a strained note in his voice.

"Probably England, Alec. Have a better chance of getting some good stock there than any place else."

"Why?"

The tall man looked down at Alec and there was a slight twinkle in his eyes. "Say, what are you driving at, Alec? As far as I know, and I've been in this business a long time, the English are pretty good at horse-breeding. Take a look at the records," he added, smiling. "You'll find I'm right."

Alec's face was serious and his gaze didn't waver. "How about the Black, sir? Do you think that he was born, well, overnight? Don't you think a horse like that . . . you said yourself that we'll probably never see another like him . . . don't you think he's the result of years and years of careful breeding?"

Mr. Volence looked at Henry and they both nodded.

Alec continued, "I don't think Abu Ishak is any

amateur at this horse-breeding business. And it just seems to me, Mr. Volence, that if I were you and so intent upon improving the blood line of the American thoroughbred, I'd skip England and go to Arabia instead and find Abu Ishak!"

Mr. Volence and Henry stared at Alec. They were silent for a minute, then Henry said, "But that's a little like trying to find a needle in a haystack, isn't it, Alec?"

"Guess so, Henry. Still, if the needle was pretty important to you, you'd probably find it." His gaze turned to Mr. Volence. "Isn't that right, sir?"

Mr. Volence didn't answer immediately. His eyes left Alec and turned toward the open field. Alec watched him anxiously.

"You may have something, Alec," he finally said.

"Maybe," Henry suggested, "the American Consulate in Arabia could help you locate Abu."

"That's an idea, Henry," Mr. Volence replied. "I wonder how much information I could dig up in Washington. Is there a phone around here?"

"You can use ours," Alec said excitedly. "C'mon."

As they climbed the steps to Alec's house, Mr. Volence asked, "Do you think Abu Ishak would sell the Black if I offered him a good price?"

"I don't think so," Alec answered, "but I'm sure you'll find that he has others he probably will sell."

Entering the house, Alec said, "Mom's out . . . the phone's in here." He led the way to it, and waited patiently while Mr. Volence asked the operator for a Washington number.

"If my Washington office can't get some information on Abu Ishak, nobody can," he explained.

A few minutes passed, then finally he got his connection.

"Flynn, this is Volence," they heard him say. "Look, I've got an important job for you to do. I want you to get all the information you can concerning an Abu Ishak . . . Ishak . . . I-S-H-A-K . . . yeah, that's it. He's in Arabia. No, I don't know where. That's what I want you to find out. That, and anything else. Use every available source. Yes, and also cable the American Consulate if you have to. I want to get in touch with Abu Ishak, if possible. No, I don't know anything about him, other than that he seems to be pretty important." There was a slight pause, then, "Sure, sure I know Arabia is a big place, but that's what you're there for. Get everything you can! And, George, listen . . . I want it within a couple of days. Something's come up and I may change my plans about going to England . . . all depends on how much information you can give me, so comb every available source. No, no . . . I won't be in New York . . . have to go back to the farm tonight to clear up some matters . . . call me there as soon as you can. Sure you've got everything straight?. . . Yeah, that's right. Okay. G'bye."

Mr. Volence turned from the telephone and joined Alec and Henry. "Well, that starts the ball rolling, and inside a couple of days I should have something."

"Then what?" Alec asked.

"Well, Alec, if there's any chance of locating Abu Ishak, I'll cable him to find out whether or not he'll sell the Black and, if not, whether he has any other horses that he'll sell. If he's receptive to my offer I'll go to Arabia on your hunch that he may be a past master at this horse-breeding game and has some horses that are worth buying. If the Black is any sample of the type of horses he's breeding I want to see the others. I'm not sure exactly what I'll do if I can't reach Abu Ishak . . . it'll all depend on how much information I can obtain as to his whereabouts. I just don't want to go to Arabia on a wild-goose chase. However, you can be sure that if there's the slightest chance of finding Abu Ishak, I'll go.''

Alec's eyes were aflame with excitement. This was the moment he'd been waiting for. "If you go . . . you wouldn't . . . what I meant to say is . . . could you use another man to help you get those horses back?''

Mr. Volence smiled. "Ah, the light dawns," he said. "Say, perhaps you saw this coming up right along. A good job of engineering, Alec." He placed a hand on his shoulder. "Seriously," he continued, "if I go, I'd like to have you come along. As you know Abu Ishak, you'd probably be able to help quite a bit.''

"Sure," Henry broke in, "and don't forget if it wasn't for Alec, the Black wouldn't be alive today. Abu knows that . . . in fact, he offered the kid a reward, but he refused it.'' Henry's gaze shifted from Mr. Volence to the brown house across the street, which could be seen through the living room window. "Couldn't use still another man, could you?" he asked anxiously.

"I could, if the other man were you, Henry, and you'd be satisfied with just expenses paid . . . no more.

"Would I!" Henry shouted. "It's a deal!"

They walked toward the door. "Well, here's hoping nothing stops us from going to Arabia," Mr. Volence said. "I'll get in touch with you as soon as I've made all arrangements. Meanwhile, Alec, you'd better speak to your parents to see if it's okay with them, so there will be no delay if we go.''

Three days later Alec received a letter from Mr. Volence, and without opening it he ran over to the barn. He found Henry cleaning the Black's bridle. "It's here!" he shouted, waving the letter in the air. They sat down on the bench and Alec tore open the envelope. "Cross your fingers, Henry," he said.

Down Under Farm
June 26th

Dear Alec and Henry,

I've exhausted all available sources and the only information that I could get concerning Abu Já Kub ben Ishak is that he's a chieftain of a small kingdom somewhere in the Kharj district, which is far to the east across the Great Central Desert of Arabia, and incidentally the least explored part of the country. There isn't a chance in the world of communicating with him, I'm afraid.

However, and Alec please note, I want to find that needle and plan to sift every piece of sand in the desert looking for it. I now definitely agree with Alec that the Black is the result of years of selective and careful breeding. Abu Ishak may have others like him.

Fortunately, an old friend of mine is now in the town of Haribwan, which is located on the western edge of the Great Central Desert. I've cabled him and he has assured me that he'll be able to get me a guide and caravan to take me across the desert. There's even the possibility that one of the traders in Haribwan may know the location of Abu Ishak's kingdom.

I'm taking quite a gamble, I know, in attempting to

locate him. Frankly, though, I'm excited about the
trip—it could be a lot of fun, and, if successful, profit-
able.

I realize, however, that with chances so slim of finding
Abu Ishak and the Black, you may not want to make this
trip with me. If not, I'll understand. But if you still want
to go, wire me immediately as I intend to leave on next
week's plane providing space is available.

Best regards,
Charles V. Volence

Alec and Henry finished reading the letter together.
"Gosh, Henry!" Alec said. "It sounds wonderful!"

"Sure does!" Henry agreed enthusiastically. "And I
have a feelin' that Volence won't leave any stone
unturned tryin' to find Abu Ishak. He's used to gettin'
what he wants." He paused, then continued, "How
about your folks, Alec . . . you said anything to them
yet?"

"Yes, Henry, I did. Told them right after Mr. Volence
was here. They didn't know what to make of it at first.
Mom's a little scared, but I think Dad's on my side.
They didn't tell me one way or another . . . whether I
could go or not, I mean. Dad said they'd let me know as
soon as Mr. Volence decided for sure he was going. I
think I can win Mom over. It's not as though I were
going alone."

Henry rose from the bench and stretched. "You're a
lot better off than I am," he said. "Haven't said a word
to the missus yet."

"What do you think she'll say, Henry?"

"Plenty," was the rueful answer.

They started walking slowly toward Henry's house.

"You going to have trouble with her?" Alec asked.

"Always have trouble," Henry replied, glancing apprehensively at the house from which came an energetic thumping and swishing and sounds of furniture being dragged. "Guess she's housecleaning."

"Maybe you ought to give a hand," Alec suggested. "It might help."

"Yeah, maybe you're right. I aim to tell her right now . . . no sense puttin' it off any longer."

Alec knocked some mud off his shoe. "Gee, Henry, I hope nothing goes wrong with either one of us. I plan to speak to Dad as soon as he gets home. I'll tell you what . . . if it's okay for you to go, whistle three times, and I'll do the same."

"Okay, Alec. Well, here's hopin' . . ." Henry turned and headed for the front door. Alec saw him stop, look down at his shoes that were caked with mud, and then go around to the back door. Grinning, Alec proceeded toward the gate and home.

As he shut the gate, he glanced nervously at his watch. It was just about time for his father to arrive home, and tonight he'd have to know whether he could go to Arabia or not. Gosh, he hoped nothing would go wrong!

As Alec crossed the street, he saw the tall figure of his father walking down from the corner bus station. He yelled and ran to meet him.

Smiling, his father removed his brown, battered hat and wiped the perspiration off his forehead. "I can hardly walk in this heat, and here you're running around like mad . . . it's good to be young!" He put an arm around Alec's shoulders and together they walked toward the house.

They were climbing the steps when Alec decided that no more time should be wasted in finding out what he had to know. "Dad," he said hesitatingly, "could I talk to you and Mother now, before dinner?"

Mr. Ramsay could tell, from the serious tone of the young voice, what his son wanted to discuss. "Sure, Alec, let's go in and get your mother out of the kitchen . . . much too hot a night to spend in there anyway."

Alec waited in the living room while his father went into the kitchen. Pretending to read the evening paper, Alec sat down in a chair. It wouldn't be long now. He'd know soon, one way or the other. . . .

His mother entered the room, wiping her hands on a short apron. Alec didn't like the stern look on his father's face. Then he smiled as he heard his father say, "Slaving over a hot stove, Alec, that's where I found her, just as I thought." He grasped his wife by the waist and they turned to Alec.

"We heard from Mr. Volence today and he's going," Alec began. "Remember, you told me to tell you when we heard from him." He stopped, looked out the window, and then back at his parents. "He's going next week and still wants me to go along."

"Henry going?" his father asked quietly, his arm still around Alec's mother.

"Think so, Dad. Sure, I'm sure he is. He told me this afternoon that he was."

His mother wasn't convinced. "Mrs. Dailey didn't mention it to me, and I saw her this afternoon," she said.

"Gosh, Mom," Alec almost shouted, "you didn't say anything to her, did you?"

"Shouldn't I?" his mother asked.

"Gee, no, Mom, Henry hasn't even . . ." Suddenly the still night was pierced by a sharp whistle. Alec turned towards the open window. The whistle was repeated twice more. "He's going, Mom," he shouted. "Yes, Henry's going!"

Mr. Ramsay smiled. "Prearranged signals, eh?" he asked. He turned to his wife, then back to Alec. "Son," he continued, "your mother and I have already decided that you can make the trip."

"Yipppeeeee!" Alec shouted, throwing his arms around them. "You're the best mother and father in the whole world."

His father laughed. "We didn't think it wise to keep a wild colt like you around here during the summer anyway."

His mother's pale blue eyes were worried. "You will be careful, Alec, won't you? And you'll do everything Mr. Volence and Henry tell you to?"

"Sure, Mom, I will . . . honest, I will. I'll be careful as I can. Why, this trip will do me worlds of good, so don't you worry. Travel is the best education a guy can get."

His father grabbed him by the belt of his trousers. "And that reminds me. Don't get back here months after everyone else has started school. Remember, you're going to college next fall."

"Sure, sure, Dad, I'll remember." He turned to his mother. "Mom, would you mind if I wired Mr. Volence before dinner? He said to wire him right away. . . . He has to get tickets on the plane. We're going by plane, Mom, think of it. I'm going to fly across the ocean, and all the way to Arabia! Gee, that'll be an education in itself, won't it, Dad! I've gotta see Henry, too. You don't mind, do you, Mom? It'll only take a few minutes, honest."

He was halfway to the door when his mother answered, her eyes on the back of his red head. "No," she said softly, "I don't mind." Her fingers tightened over the large hand around her waist.

Arabia Bound

4

Alec, Henry and Mr. Volence waited impatiently for
their flight to be called at La Guardia's Marine Air
Terminal. Through the window Alec could see the giant
flying boat cabled securely against the ramp that led out
over Flushing Bay. His heart pounded, for it would be
only a short time now before they'd be on her . . . and
off! "That's the *Flying Clipper,* isn't it, Mr. Volence?"
he asked excitedly.

"Yes, Alec, that's what they call it. She's a beauty,
isn't she?"

"Sure is," Alec agreed. "We ought to be off soon."
His eyes swept to the clock. Seven o'clock, and they
were scheduled to leave at seven-thirty. He turned to
the window again and looked at the clear, blue sky
overhead. It was going to be a nice day, and they were
sure to take off unless there was "dirty" weather over

the Atlantic. Mr. Volence had told him that the ship wouldn't leave unless weather reports were good. He hoped nothing would prevent them from going today. He'd looked forward to this day ever so much, and didn't want to put it off any longer.

Henry caught him looking out the window. "We'll take off all right, Alec," he assured him. "They'd have told us earlier if the weather was no good over the Atlantic." He jerked his head in the direction of the adjoining room. "C'mon. They have some vittles inside, and my stomach's cryin' from hunger."

"Didn't you have breakfast home, Henry? I did."

"Naw, I didn't even wake the missus," and Henry smiled. "'Fraid she'd change her mind at the last minute. Better to go hungry."

Mr. Volence was busy and told them he'd join them in a few minutes. Henry and Alec made their way to the table where the other passengers were having breakfast. To Alec they all looked as though they were accustomed to transatlantic travel. Most of them were casually reading the morning papers, patiently waiting for the time to embark.

Alec was too excited to eat anything, but Henry had two orders of ham and eggs. "Nothin' like a full stomach." He grinned.

"Sure, nothin' like it," Alec agreed, glancing out the window at the great silver bird he'd soon be on. The morning sun reflected from its hull and shone in his eyes. He turned back to Henry. "You never told me how you managed to get away, Henry. Did you have much trouble?"

Henry answered between mouthfuls. "A little. She

couldn't see it at first, but then I told her I'd bring her back a lot of ivory . . . she's crazy about ivory . . . has all sorts of junkets and trinkets around the house.''

"But, Henry, there isn't much ivory in Arabia.''

"No?''

"No.''

"Well,'' Henry said after a pause, "I'll just have to get some somewhere.'' He swallowed his coffee. "Anyway, her sister from the Ozarks is gonna spend the summer with us, same as she did last year and the year before, and she always sleeps in my bed. So it's just as well that I'm not around.''

Mr. Volence arrived and sat down with them. "I'll just have a cup of coffee,'' he said, "I've had breakfast.'' He glanced at the clock. ". . . almost time,'' he added.

"Is that the crew over there?'' Alec asked, nodding toward a table in one corner of the room at which a group of men, wearing dark blue uniforms, was seated.

"Yes, it is,'' Mr. Volence replied.

"Gee, it's a big crew,'' Alec said. "There are twelve.''

"It takes a good many men to handle these babies.''

A bell rang twice and Alec saw the crew leave their table and walk toward the door. He rose from his seat. Why weren't the others getting up? They'd be late.

"Sit down, Alec,'' and Mr. Volence smiled, "the next bell will be ours. The crew has to warm the ship up a bit before we take over.''

Alec watched the crew as they went down the long runway, and onto the ramp that led to the plane. They marched in a column of twos.

"That's the captain and the first officer up front, Alec," Mr. Volence told him.

"There are almost as many crew members as there are passengers," Henry commented.

A few minutes later there was a loud roar as the four engines were started. The propellers whirled in the sun and Alec felt a tingling sensation go over him. He glanced at the clock . . . just a few minutes more. He thought of his mother and father on the upper observation deck waiting for him to depart from the building and board the ship. He wondered if they felt the same as he did.

Five minutes passed, and then the roar of the engines rose to a higher pitch. Still there was no signal for the passengers to board. Alec became a little panicky. Supposing something was wrong with one of the engines and they didn't go! Then the bell rang again. "That's us!" he shouted. He rose to his feet so hastily that he tipped the long table, upsetting a cup of coffee into a matronly woman's lap. Sputtering an apology, he ran for the door, closely followed by Mr. Volence, Henry and the other passengers.

They walked down the runway and onto the ramp. Turning, Alec looked up at the observation deck of the Administration Building. "Look!" he shouted. "There's Mother and Dad." Alec and Henry waved.

"Have a good trip," Alec's father called. His mother waved a small handkerchief.

"So long!" Alec yelled above the roar of the plane's engines.

They were alongside the *Flying Clipper* now and some of the passengers had already boarded the ship. She strained the steel cables that held her to the ramp, as though impatient to be in flight.

Alec took one final look at his parents, waved again, and then climbed down the passageway, followed by Henry and Mr. Volence.

Inside, Alec was amazed to find how spacious the plane was. The steward showed them to their compartment, and Mr. Volence told Alec to sit by the large porthole. Henry took the seat opposite Alec and Mr. Volence sat down beside him.

They were on the opposite side of the ramp, so Alec was not able to see the Administration Building or his mother and father. "You'll be able to see them when we taxi out of the bay into the channel," Mr. Volence assured him.

The plane's engines slowed to idling speed, and the steward returned and helped them fasten their seat belts. "We'll be taking off in a few minutes," he told them. "We're waiting for one more passenger who is to occupy this space." He nodded to the empty seat beside Alec.

"I was of the opinion the *Flying Clipper* didn't wait for anyone." Mr. Volence smiled.

The steward snapped Alec's seat belt. "We don't usually," he replied, ". . . but we've had orders to wait. He'll be here in a few minutes. He's in the customs office now."

Alec looked out the window across the dark waters of the bay. A little to the right he could see La Guardia Airport and the commercial airline planes taking off. He and his father had spent many a Sunday afternoon there and once they had flown from La Guardia to Florida to spend the Christmas vacation with his mother's sister. Only once, though, had he been lucky enough to catch a flying boat taking off from the bay bound on a long journey across the ocean. He'd never forget that great silver bird streaking down the channel, leaving a white, rolling wake behind.

"I believe this seat is mine?" a voice with a decidedly foreign accent asked. Alec turned and stared at the man standing in the aisle. He was a short man with tremendous shoulders and a bull neck. His face, so dark that it was almost black, was round and deeply furrowed. Small gray eyes squinted from sunken black pits that wrinkled at the corners as though he had spent much time in the bright sun.

He had removed his hat and was wiping his bald head with a purple handkerchief. It was then that Alec noticed the left sleeve hanging empty beside him. Alec felt a surge of pity go through him. Instinctively he had taken a dislike to the man's looks, but the thought of going through life with only one arm made him feel sorry for him. He jumped to his feet and removed the newspapers and magazines that he had left on the unoccupied seat. "Here, sir," he said, moving closer to the window to give the stranger more room.

Nodding, the man carefully lowered his heavy body into the seat. After he had settled himself he looked directly at Mr. Volence and said, "Allow me to introduce myself. My name is Ibn al Khaldun." He smiled and his mouth was toothless.

Mr. Volence acknowledged the introduction and then presented Henry and Alec. When Alec grasped the pudgy hand he found it cold and clammy.

The plane's engines were revved up and Alec heard the men on the ramp removing the cables which held the ship. Forgetting the stranger beside him, he said to Henry excitedly, "This is it!" Then he pushed his face up against the window.

As the plane began to move, the steward said, "Please make certain all seat belts are securely fastened." Alec checked his, and then noticed that Ibn al Khaldun was attempting to fasten his belt with one hand. "Here, sir," he said, "let me help you."

Perspiration ran down in rivulets on the man's fat face. "Thank you, no," and he grinned. "It isn't necessary. You see, one gets accustomed to accomplishing many feats with one hand . . . when he has only one." Snapping the belt, he leaned back in the seat, and closed his eyes.

The silver plane taxied away from the ramp, and Alec was able to see his mother and father still standing on the observation deck. He waved, but realized they weren't able to see him. The plane turned and headed across the bay toward the channel. As the figures of his parents faded from view, Alec felt a wave of homesickness come over him. He watched the water swish by and thought how much he'd miss his mother and father.

The sudden splash of mounting water against the window startled Alec. The plane's engines had risen to a mighty roar. Suddenly he realized that they were in the channel and taking off! Alec watched the landscape on the other side of the water speed past with lightning swiftness. Faster and faster they went until white foam completely blocked his vision and he could no longer see even the large wing or pontoon.

Mr. Volence watched Alec's tense face and smiled. "It'll be clear in a few minutes," he assured him. "The steward told me that we have a capacity load and that requires a long run. Remember, too, that a baby like this carries around four thousand gallons of gas."

"Gee, it's a wonder they ever get off," Alec said, watching the water cascade down the window. "It's like being under a waterfall."

The engines roared to a new, higher pitch and suddenly the window cleared. Alec watched as the silver hull broke away from the water. "We're off!" he yelled. The fat figure of Ibn al Khaldun stirred at the sound of Alec's voice. His beady eyes opened, turned toward Alec, and then closed again.

The plane began a gradual ascent. Below, Alec could see the Administration Building, La Guardia Airport, and not far away, Flushing. He looked for his house and found it. The plane circled and then headed out over Long Island and toward the sea, its silver wings shining in the early morning sun.

The next few hours passed quickly, and before Alec knew it the steward was serving lunch. They were well out of sight of land and headed south for their first stop which, he had been told by Mr. Volence, would be Port of Spain, Trinidad. They would spend the night there and the next day take off for Natal, Brazil, the last stop before they flew over the Atlantic to Africa.

Alec looked across at Henry, and knew from the intense expression on his face that he was enjoying the trip as much as he. Mr. Volence was busy eating his cold ham and potato salad while attempting to read his magazine. Ibn al Khaldun had not desired any lunch and was again sleeping. Deep, guttural snores escaped from his throat. Alec finished eating and turned to the window.

They were over the Gulf Stream and the water was a deep azure blue. Soft wisps of clouds passed between them and the ocean below, and the steady hum of the engines made Alec sleepy. He looked forward at the two propellers on his side flashing in the sun, and the long wing extending far out to one side. He closed his eyes and let his head rest against the back of his seat. A few minutes later he was asleep.

The sun was low over the water when he awakened. Sleepily, he opened his eyes and found Henry and Mr. Volence smiling at him.

"Good nap?" Mr. Volence inquired.

"Gee, yes," Alec replied. "It must have been a long one, too!"

Henry snorted. "It surely was. Say, maybe about three hours."

Alec looked out the window and, glancing down, saw small submerged beds of coral under the water. "Coral reefs," he said. "We must be pretty far south. Do you know about where, Mr. Volence?"

"No, but we can ask the steward. He'll know." He called the steward over and was told that they were only a half-hour away from Port of Spain.

"We should be able to see the coastline in a few minutes then," Mr. Volence told them.

"That's pretty good traveling," Alec said. "Breakfast in New York and dinner in South America."

The steward smiled. "Scheduled flying time is eleven hours and we usually hit it right on the button," he said.

"It's from Port of Spain to Natal that the trip's the toughest. We'll buck head winds all the way tomorrow."

"Will we leave pretty early in the morning?" Alec asked.

"Six o'clock. If we're lucky we'll make Natal in about fifteen hours, which means about nine at night. The following day we hop the Atlantic to a place called Fish Lake in Liberia. Ever hear of it?"

"No," Alec answered, "but it sounds interesting." He paused a moment. "Say," he continued, "you mentioned that we land at Natal at nine . . . that is, if we're lucky . . . and it should be dark by that time. Can you land these ships at night without any trouble?"

"We usually manage." The steward smiled. "Of course our pilot has to be careful not to hit any crocodiles or floating logs, but other than that there's nothing to it. You'll see how he does it when we come into Natal tomorrow night." His eyes shifted to the window. "There's the northern coast of Trinidad now. It'll only be a matter of minutes before we're at our base. Better put a few things in your overnight bag." He put his hand on Ibn al Khaldun's shoulder and shook him gently. The Arab's eyes opened quickly. "Port of Spain, sir," the steward told him. Sluggishly Ibn al Khaldun straightened in his seat. He dismissed the steward with a quick jerk of his hand.

Alec felt his dislike for this man grow more and more intense. It was obvious that he did not want to talk to them, and Alec had no intention of encouraging conversation. Ibn al Khaldun zipped his overnight bag shut and then stared vacantly over Mr. Volence's head, ignoring them all.

Alec turned to the window again. They were only a short distance away from the coast and the plane was gradually descending. The pressure in his eardrums increased and he felt a twinge of pain. He chewed his gum vigorously to relieve the pressure.

"Try swallowing a few times, Alec," Mr. Volence advised.

A few minutes later they were over the beach and following a small river that wound its way back toward towering cliffs. Alec wondered why the pilot was flying so low . . . too low to make the cliffs ahead. Then he saw the opening through which the river passed, and the large bay beyond. The plane swooped through the break in the cliffs and swiftly descended toward the water. As the silver hull creased the bay, sheets of white foam again covered the window. Gradually, as the ship slowed, the window became clear and Alec could see the pier toward which they were taxiing. A short distance beyond was a low rambling building perched on many long poles, giving it the appearance of a giant centipede.

A little later, after having passed through customs, they were speeding toward the town of Port of Spain. The airline had provided two cars to take the passengers to the hotel and Alec was glad to note that Ibn al Khaldun was not in theirs. "He certainly is an unpleasant guy to have around," he commented to Henry.

"Yeah, he's not what you'd call sociable," agreed Henry. "Tried to make conversation with him back there, but he wouldn't have much of it." He paused for a moment, pondered and then continued, "Funny, though, come to think of it. He knew an awful lot about me and the horses I've trained; he opened up a little when I mentioned Chang and the Derby back in '32. He said he thought Prince Pat, the young colt I told you about who fell in his second race and had to be done away with, was a better horse than Chang and the fastest horse I'd ever had. Funny thing about that is I thought so, too, but never mentioned it; furthermore, very few people ever heard of Prince Pat as I hadn't had him ready for big racing at the time of his accident. These Arabs are sure peculiar people.''

Early the next morning they were on their way again. Ibn al Khaldun, who the steward told them was also going to Arabia, had changed his seat for one nearer the front of the plane, claiming that riding near the tail made him ill. "Good riddance," muttered Alec to himself.

Hour after hour the silver plane bucked the strong head winds which swept north up the coast of South America. They flew over dense green jungle country and Alec, looking down, wondered how they'd ever be found if the engines failed and they had to land. It was dark, unexplored country, alive with many terrors.

The sun passed overhead and descended rapidly in the west. Glancing at his watch, Alec found that it was after seven and realized that soon it would be dark. He looked ahead, hoping to see Natal, although he realized that they were not scheduled to arrive until after nine o'clock. Only a greenish-black carpet extended to the horizon. He let his head fall back on his seat and thought about Ibn al Khaldun. Funny he should know so much about Henry and American racehorses. Still, since he was an Arab, it was in all probability only natural that he should take an interest in American racing. He was an odd guy. Repulsive-looking, too, with his bald head and swarthy, fat face. Alec's conscience bothered him as he remembered Ibn al Khaldun's empty sleeve. It was tough to go through life handicapped that way. Perhaps he was mistaken about him. Perhaps it was just a case of not knowing him well enough. Still, there was something. . . .

The plane flew on, and eventually Alec's thoughts turned from Ibn al Khaldun to the Black and the search ahead. Would they be lucky enough to locate the kingdom of Abu Já Kub ben Ishak? He repeated the name of the Black's owner again . . . Abu Já Kub ben Ishak. It was important that he remember that name; he had said it over and over again since Abu had departed with the Black. That was the only clue they had to the stallion's whereabouts; that, and the knowledge that Abu lived in the least explored district of Arabia, the Kharj district, far to the east across the Great Central Desert. It wasn't much. Alec closed his eyes and thought about his horse.

The steward awakened Alec sometime later. "You were interested in night landings yesterday," he said. "It'll only be a few minutes. You can see the lights of Natal just ahead."

Sleepily, Alec flattened his nose against the window. It was very dark and they were quite low. Below he could just make out a long, winding river which they were following. He turned toward Henry and Mr. Volence and noticed that they were fastening their seat belts. Drawing his own tightly about him, he said, "This is going to be good. How in the devil will he be able to see? That's a river, isn't it? Is he going to land in it?"

"That's the River do Norte," Mr. Volence explained. "The base is on it, and if you look a few miles ahead you'll be able to see the landing lights which will guide the pilot in making his landing."

Alec again turned to the window. Ahead, as Mr. Volence had said, was a string of lights on the river. There were seven groups of them and each group was a small, circular glowing ring. The one nearest the plane was red, but all the others were green. "The pilot will land alongside them," Mr. Volence explained, "just to the right. Watch."

The plane was now nearing the group of red lights. Alec peered into the inky darkness of the jungle on the other side of the river. They were coming in fast and just over the river. Sweeping past the red lights, the silver bird struck the water and proceeded swiftly up the line.

Henry sat back in his seat and relaxed. "Nothin' to it," he mumbled.

At the base they went through the same procedure as at Port of Spain, and then were sped away to Natal to spend the night. "Tomorrow," Alec reminded Henry, "it's Africa!" They were well on their way to the home of the Black!

The following days proved monotonous to all the passengers except Alec and Henry. Together they shared the thrill of flying the Atlantic for the first time. Before nightfall they were on the African continent and based at Fish Lake, Liberia. Their next hop took them to Lagos, Nigeria, and then came Leopoldville, deep in the heart of the Belgian Congo. The following day they took off for their final destination, Aden, Arabia.

As they flew over a barren African plain, Alec's thoughts turned to the trip ahead. According to Mr.

Volence they were to take a train from Aden to Haribwan, which was located just southwest of the Great Central Desert. It was there that they would meet Mr. Volence's friend, who had assured them that he would be able to acquire a caravan and a guide to take them across the desert.

It was late afternoon when the steward touched Alec on the shoulder. "There's the Bab el Mandeb," he said, pointing to a large expanse of water ahead. "It's just a short hop across to Arabia, so we'll be in Aden in less than a half-hour."

"Are we the only ones getting off there?" Alec asked, nodding toward his friends.

"On the contrary, practically all the passengers are bound for Aden. We'll take on some more there tomorrow, and then it's Cairo and across the northern coast of Africa to Morocco. We'll be back at La Guardia inside of six days with any luck at all."

"That's certainly getting around to a lot of places," Alec said.

Soon they had left Africa behind and were crossing the channel of Bab el Mandeb. "It connects the Gulf of Aden and the Red Sea," Alec explained to Henry. He had been through it twice, as his ships had taken that route to and from Bombay, India, when he had visited his Uncle Ralph. As Alec's thoughts turned to the *Drake* and that disastrous home voyage, he became depressed. To think that only he and a few others had been rescued of all the passengers and crew. And little had they known what was ahead of them when they had docked at Aden.

He could see the white buildings of the city ahead. His

gaze turned northward, for it would be that direction in which they would go.

The plane circled slowly above its base. "Well, here we are," mumbled Henry.

Mr. Volence, winking at Alec, said, "Only the beginning, Henry. We won't waste much time in Aden . . . try to catch the first train to Haribwan that we can get. After just sitting all this time, I'm itching to pick up the trail."

"The trail of the Black," added Alec. He paused, then added confidently, "We'll find him."

"I wish I could share your optimism, Alec," Mr. Volence said. "However, I can assure you that we won't leave Arabia until we've made a thorough search."

They were coming in now, and the plane glided smoothly toward the water. The silver hull cut the channel and the water streamed up and covered the window. A few minutes later they were taxiing to the dock. As the plane was cabled, the passengers rose from their seats, each concerned with his own business. For days they had lived in a small confined world of their own, but now it had ended and they were eager to get along.

After passing though the customs, Alec and his companions awaited the car which would take them to their hotel. Ibn al Khaldun came out of the building and headed for a black sedan. He was wearing a white suit and shirt, open at the neck. His bald head was bare. Stopping, he withdrew a white silk handkerchief from his coat pocket and wiped the rivulets of perspiration from his face. His gaze turned toward them, and then he walked slowly in their direction.

"Wonder what the devil he wants?" Alec said softly.

"Probably going to bid us a fond farewell," muttered Henry.

Ibn al Khaldun stopped in front of them, but didn't speak. Finally Mr. Volence, to break the silence, said, "Is your home in Aden, Mr. Khaldun?"

The Arab's gaze shifted from Alec to Mr. Volence. A few seconds passed before he replied, "No. My home is far to the north."

Alec asked, "Anywhere near the Great Central Desert?"

Ibn al Khaldun's beady eyes shifted again to Alec. A slight smile was on his lips, disclosing the toothless gums. He nodded but did not say a word.

Mr. Volence and Henry watched Alec, for they knew the next question the boy would ask.

"Have you by any chance ever heard of a man named Abu Já Kub ben Ishak?" Alec asked.

Ibn al Khaldun ran the silk handkerchief across his face and then wiped the top of his skull before shaking his head negatively. "Arabia is a large and most complex country," he replied softly, his words heavily accented. "One does not have many acquaintances in the north." He had left the handkerchief on the top of his head and Alec was thinking how ridiculous it looked, when a slight breeze blew it to the ground in front of him. Alec bent to pick it up.

Ibn al Khaldun had also bent down to retrieve his handkerchief. Alec had his hand on the silk cloth, when he stopped short. In front of him, dangling from the Arab's bare neck, was a gold chain on which hung a medallion . . . that of a bird with wings outstretched in flight.

The Phoenix

5

It was not until a few minutes later, after Ibn al Khaldun had left, that Alec told Henry and Mr. Volence what he had seen.

"Are you sure it was the same medallion?" Henry asked, his voice tense.

Alec dug a hand into his coat pocket and withdrew the gold chain. "It was the very same, Henry . . . just like this one. I couldn't be mistaken!"

Mr. Volence's eyes swept to the black limousine into which Ibn al Khaldun had disappeared. "Come on! Let's trail him." He hailed a cab and the three climbed into it just as the car ahead pulled away from the curb.

Mr. Volence instructed the driver to keep about a hundred yards behind. "All we want to do," he explained to Alec, "is to find out where he's staying, then we'll inform the police."

"But we really haven't any case," Alec said. "It'll just be his word against ours."

"Yes, I know. We might be able to learn something, though, that'll help us. I have a few friends in the government here who might be able to throw a scare into him. I'm sure we couldn't get any satisfaction out of Ibn al Khaldun ourselves. It's our only chance."

They were near the outskirts of the city when Alec noticed that the distance between the two cars was increasing. "We'll have to step on it," he said, "or we'll lose him."

The black car suddenly turned from the main road down a narrow side street. It had slowed down a bit, and the taxi driver had no trouble keeping behind. They went around the block and then arrived back on the main road.

"That's funny," Henry mused.

"Not so funny," Alec said. "He wanted to find out whether or not he was being followed, and we walked right into it."

Bending forward, Mr. Volence told the driver to increase his speed. I'm afraid you're right, Alec. He's stepping on it, and we'll be lucky if we can keep up with him."

Ibn al Khaldun's car swept along the highway, and in a few minutes it was obvious to all that the broken-down cab in which they were riding could not possibly keep up with the car ahead.

Ibn al Khaldun was out of sight when they reached the city limits.

"Anyway," Alec said, "that proves he had something

to do with the attack on the Black, and knew that we were suspicious of him, or he would have stopped instead of running away.''

''Not necessarily,'' Mr. Volence suggested. ''It might be something else. . . .''

Alec was unconvinced. ''I have his car's license number, anyway,'' he told them. ''We can check at the police station.''

''Good boy!'' Mr. Volence said.

A few minutes later, the cab pulled up in front of the station and Mr. Volence went inside while Alec and Henry waited in the cab. He returned shortly afterward. ''Not much luck, unfortunately,'' he told them. ''The car belongs to a rental agency and the driver was ordered to report at the airport to meet Ibn al Khaldun. I'm going to call them again a little later and they'll let me know the address to which the driver took our friend. We still may be able to learn something.''

After they had checked in at their hotel, Mr. Volence called the car rental agency only to find that Ibn al Khaldun had dismissed the car and driver soon after they had reached the city limits. The driver had informed the agency that his fare had hailed a cab immediately after dismissing him.

The following day Mr. Volence talked to some business associates about Ibn al Khaldun, but learned little. ''They told me,'' he informed Alec and Henry later back at the hotel, ''that there are many families by the name of Khaldun in the central and north country, and that it would be a waste of time attempting to track him down.''

Henry rubbed a large hand over his two-day beard. "Guess the only thing we can do is to trek on, keepin' our eyes open for him."

"I have a feeling he'll turn up again," Alec mused.

The next day they set out for Haribwan. As they awaited their train at the station, Mr. Volence told them that he had telephoned his friend in Haribwan, and that he was expecting them.

"Has he been able to get us a guide?" Alec asked.

"No, unfortunately. He said it wouldn't be any trouble to get a guide to take us across the desert, but going into the mountains is another story. Seems it's dangerous country, as there are many hostile tribes and few men have ventured into it."

Henry grimaced. "You don't make it sound too good," he said.

The train, with antiquated engine and wooden cars, pulled laboriously into the station. They found their seats and settled back for the ride.

"How long a trip is it?" Alec asked.

"A little over twelve hours," Mr. Volence replied. He glanced at his watch. "We should arrive in Haribwan a little after eight tonight."

The heat was intense and Alec covered his face with his handkerchief. Henry and Mr. Volence removed their jackets. Soon the train was on its way, and a dry breeze swept through the car.

"I guess this must be one of the hottest countries in the world," Alec murmured.

"It is," Mr. Volence agreed with a smile, "and the driest. But we'd better get used to it."

Alec looked out the open window at the steppe-like tracts covered with small bushes. To the west he could see the coastal mountains gradually rising as they swept to the north. Occasionally he could see a small farm with cultivated land.

"The west and northern coasts of Arabia are the most fertile," Mr. Volence explained. "To the east is only the Great Central Desert and the mountains toward which we're headed. Some Arabs call their country an island, surrounded by water on three sides and sand on the fourth. Geologists say," he added after a minute's pause, "that Arabia once joined the natural continuation of the Sahara, now separated by the rift of the Nile Valley and the great chasm of the Red Sea."

"Aren't there any rivers at all? Alec asked.

"None of any significance," Mr. Volence told him. "There is a network of wadis, depressions in the surface, which fill with water, but only periodically, during the short rainy season."

"At that rate, I don't see how they can grow much. What do they eat?"

"It's true there's little tillable land, Alec. But on the coastal areas they have dates, coconut palms, grapes, and numerous fruits as well as almonds, sugar cane and watermelons. They also have sheep and goats. Their coffee, too, is the finest in the world. In the desert, I suppose, the chief items on the nomad's menu are dates and milk."

Henry, very much interested in the conversation, muttered, "Dates and milk . . . that's something to look forward to."

As the hours passed and the train wound its way to the

northeast, the country became less populated and the terrain more grim. Great sandy wastes spread before them. Barely visible now were the mountains to the west. Alec's gaze swept over the other passengers in the car, most of whom were sleeping. There were a few, presumably British from their features, dressed in clothes like his own. But the majority were Arabs, wearing long white skirts with a sash and a flowing upper garment, which pictures had made familiar to Alec. Most of them wore a shawl held by a cord over their heads. They were of middle stature, of powerful build, and to Alec their features, characterized by a broad jaw, aquiline nose and flat cheeks, expressed dignity and pride. He could not help but think how little they looked like Ibn al Khaldun with his fat, evil face.

The medallion dangling in Mr. Volence's hand attracted Alec's attention. Noticing how closely he was scrutinizing it, he asked, "Any new clues?"

Mr. Volence did not answer for several seconds, then he looked up and met Alec's intense gaze. "I was just thinking about something one of my friends in Aden mentioned yesterday about this," he said. "He happens to be quite a student of mythology, and thought that this resembled the fabulous bird of Egypt, the Phoenix. But neither he nor I have ever seen a drawing of the Phoenix such as this one, with its wings outstretched in flight. Still, I can see what he means . . ."

"The Phoenix? What's the story?" Alec asked.

"Briefly," Mr. Volence replied, "the Phoenix was probably the aspect of the sun god and as such was worshipped. According to legend, it lived five hundred years in Arabia. The story goes that when the Phoenix finally felt life ebbing away, it laid an egg in its nest and set fire to it. Thus, it burned to death but out of the ashes a new Phoenix came to life. It represented the resurrection of the dead.''

"Gee, that's interesting," Alec said. "But if it is the Phoenix, what do you think it symbolizes to Ibn al Khaldun?''

"I haven't the slightest idea, Alec," Mr. Volence answered. "Perhaps nothing . . . maybe just a piece he carries around.''

Henry, who had been listening intently to the conversation, joined in. "It's a secret order, or somethin', I'll bet." His large hand dropped on Alec's leg, and he continued. "So far as we know there are two of these things, the one you have and the one around Ibn's fat neck. Now, if he didn't try to kill the Black that night, someone else wearing the bird did, which means there's some sort of an organization or somethin'.''

"Or," Alec added, "if Ibn al Khaldun did attack the Black he had another medallion.''

"Well," Mr. Volence said, "it's something to think about. When we get to Haribwan, maybe Coggins will be able to help.''

Haribwan

6

It was almost dark when they arrived at Haribwan. As Alec reached up to the rack for his suitcase, he felt a renewed excitement. For Haribwan was really the beginning of their search for the Black. To the north and east was the desert, void of civilization. Haribwan was their last outpost. No longer would they be able to depend upon commercial means of traveling or hotel accommodations, for when they left this small Arabian town they would be on their own.

The other passengers left the train and Henry, Mr. Volence and Alec followed.

Outside, vendors shouted forth their wares to the new arrivals, their voices raised to the highest pitch in competition with the incessant tramp of passers-by and a multitude of donkeys and camels laden with the varied products of the desert and farms. The air was charged

with every conceivable odor, and Alec sniffed sensi-
tively.

Mr. Volence spied his friend Coggins. "Bruce!" he
shouted. "It's good to see you."

A tall man with thinning white hair, wearing large
horn-rimmed spectacles, grasped Mr. Volence's outstretched hand. "Charlie, you old blighter you," he said
enthusiastically, "it's been a long time."

Mr. Volence introduced Henry and Alec and then
they made their way through the crowd. "Must be over
ten years that you've lived here, isn't it, Bruce?" Mr.
Volence asked.

"Thirteen or fourteen years, I think it is. You lose
track of time here."

Mr. Volence turned to Henry and Alec. "Coggins,
here," he explained, "was sent by his company to do a
temporary job in Haribwan, which was to have lasted a
month at the most. He's been here ever since."

"I made it a permanent job," Mr. Coggins explained,
smiling. "This place grows on one, you know."

"It must," Mr. Volence said. "I recall the letter that
you wrote just before you left England on this deal. You
weren't very happy about it. Remember?"

"I most certainly do," Mr. Coggins said. "But," and
his voice became earnest, "these people, the country
. . . well, it's difficult to explain how I feel. You'll find
out for yourself, in time. Those who have never been
here think of Arabia as a harsh and forbidding land, but
it's really warm and hospitable."

"It's warm all right," Henry muttered, wiping his
brow.

Finally they arrived at Mr. Coggins' car, an early

model Ford. "I'm afraid I can't accommodate you with any better means of traveling. Still, it will get us there." He patted the hood cherishingly.

"I'm surprised to see you have a car," Mr. Volence said.

"There are a few of them around. But come, let's be on our way."

Mr. Coggins drove the car slowly through the crowded, narrow streets of the town. "Auto traffic is rare here," he said, "and I always have to be careful. The people really resent motor vehicles, feeling that the donkey, camel and horse are adequate means of transportation. I only use the car on rare occasions such as this." He was smiling.

Alec kept busy watching the passing scene. He noticed several men in European dress, but the majority were clothed in the white flowing raiment of the desert. "Are there many Europeans here?" he asked.

"No, not many," Mr. Coggins replied. "The natives call them *Ifranji,* or Frank."

Alec saw a few women, all veiled, walking along the streets; others peeped through the latticed windows of their homes as the car went by.

Suddenly they came upon a large group of people standing in front of an impressive-looking building of white stone. Mr. Coggins brought the car to a stop. "The evening call to prayer," he said. "That's the mosque, the Moslem place of worship. Look up on the tower, the minaret it's called, and you can see the muezzin, or crier, summoning the Moslems to prayer."

Alec's gaze followed Mr. Coggins' pointed finger. The slender, lofty tower was attached to the mosque and surrounded by a projecting balcony upon which a man in a white robe was standing. Then his voice descended upon the multitude: *"La ilaha illa-'llah: Muhammadum rasulu-'llah,"* he cried reverently.

"It means 'No God but Allah: Mohammed is the messenger of Allah,'" Mr. Coggins explained. "No sentence is more often repeated in Arabia. These are the first words to strike the ear of the new-born Moslem child, and the last to be uttered at the grave. Five times a day . . . at dawn, midday, mid-afternoon, sunset, and nightfall . . . the words are chanted by the muezzin in prayer from the tops of the minarets throughout Arabia."

The muezzin's voice prayed on, echoed by the voices of the faithful below. It was an impressive spectacle and the occupants of the car remained silent.

Later, when the prayers had ended, they moved on, and soon arrived at the home of Mr. Coggins. The door to the house opened into a courtyard, and Alec, who had been unimpressed by what he had seen of the house from the street, found himself pleasantly surprised. In the center, among a group of small orange trees, was a large fountain which jetted a veil-like spray of water high in the air. The rooms surrounded the courtyard and above the iron balcony on the second floor was an overhanging cloister which kept the sun's rays from the rooms.

Mr. Coggins showed them to their rooms and told them dinner would be served as soon as they were ready.

Alec, who had a room all to himself, washed in a large basin. The oil lamp cast eerie flickering shadows on the walls, and his thoughts turned to home. Here he was, almost halfway around the world from his mother and father. He wondered what they were doing, and how long it would be before he would see them again. True, he was supposed to be back in a few months, but he sensed now more than ever before the hazardous nature of the task that lay ahead. This had all been a dream a few short weeks ago, but now it was very much of a reality. Would they be able to get a guide? If so, would they find the home of Abu Já Kub ben Ishak and the Black?

Alec finished washing and left the room. The sound of voices led him to a large room, in the center of which was a long table laden with an assortment of fruits. Mr. Volence and Henry were talking to their host.

Mr. Coggins smiled at Alec. "Now that we're all here let's sit down to dinner. I'm sure you must be very hungry." He rang a small bell on the table and almost immediately a tall, brown-skinned youth of about Alec's age entered the room bearing a steaming dish of food. He set the dish down in front of Mr. Coggins and then stepped behind him, his brown, almost liquid eyes burning with curiosity. His gaze swept around the table and finally came to rest on Alec.

"This is Raj, my houseboy," Mr. Coggins explained, looking up over his shoulder and smiling. "Raj, these are my good friends, Mr. Volence, Mr. Dailey, and Alec Ramsay."

The Arabian youth bent his erect, big-boned figure from the waist. "How do you do," he said softly, and each word was pronounced and clipped. "It is indeed very fine to have you with us." Then he left the room, walking with long and graceful strides.

After Raj had left the room, Mr. Volence said, "He speaks English very well. Has he been with you long, Bruce?"

"Yes, a very long time," Mr. Coggins replied quietly. "Not long after I arrived here, I was asked by a good friend of mine, a trader, who spent most of his time in the desert, if I would take care of Raj for him while he was away. Raj was about three at the time. . . . Raj was not his son, although he loved him as one. It seems that on one of his trips across the desert my friend found this baby . . . alone . . . on a small oasis. Obviously, he had been left there to die by someone, but fortunately my friend arrived before it was too late. He brought him back to Haribwan."

"The trader, your friend, does he come back often?" Henry asked.

"No." Mr. Coggins paused. "He never returned from his last trip . . . that was at least nine years ago. Part of his caravan returned. They had been attacked by desert raiders, and the few who got back were very fortunate."

"A very interesting story," Mr. Volence said. "You have no clues as to the identity of the child?"

"No, nothing. The baby's clothes were very well woven and of fine quality, indicating that his parents, whoever they might have been, were wealthy." Mr. Coggins paused while he passed some dried meat to Henry, then continued. "Raj is happy, I'm sure. I've tutored him, and he's been very quick to learn. I've told him his story, and knowing there's no possible way of learning the identity of his parents, he's content, although I assume it's always more or less in the back of his mind."

Henry, after emptying his glass of fruit juice, asked, "Those desert raiders you spoke about . . . are they still pretty active?"

"Yes, Henry, and I'm afraid they always will be," he replied. "Let me tell you a little about them . . . it's something you should know."

Mr. Coggins pushed his plate forward and removed his spectacles. "The original Arabs," he continued, "were the Bedouins, who refer to themselves as 'people of the camel.' Now in the fertile lands to the north, west and south, empires have come and gone, but to the east, in the barren wastes of the Rub' al Khali, which you call the Great Central Desert, the Bedouin has remained forever the same. He is no gypsy, roaming aimlessly for the sake of roaming. Wherever he goes, he goes seeking pasture for his sheep- and camel-raising, horse-breeding, hunting . . . and raiding. Strange as this may sound to you, raiding is one of the few manly occupations accepted by the Bedouins. An early Arabian poet once wrote: 'Our business is to make raids on the enemy, on our neighbor and on our own brother, in case we find none to raid but a brother!"

Mr. Coggins emptied his glass and then went on. "The Bedouin, his horse, and camel rule supreme in the desert. His tenacity and endurance have enabled him to survive where almost everything else perishes. Yes, and he still lives as his forefathers did, in tents of goats' or camels' hair, and grazes his sheep and goats in the same ancient pastures. The nomad of the desert is a bundle of nerves, bones and sinews. Dates and milk are the chief items on his menu."

"No solid foods at all?" Mr. Volence interrupted.

"Dates and camel flesh are probably his only solid foods," Mr Coggins replied. "Incidentally, the Bedouin considers the camel a 'special gift of Allah.' He feasts on its flesh, covers himself with its skin, makes his tent of its hair, and uses its dung as fuel. It is his constant companion, his means of transportation, his wealth and his blood."

Having listened very intently, Alec broke in, "But his horse. I've always thought that that was his most valued possession."

"It is, Alec," agreed Mr. Coggins with a smile. "But it is an animal of luxury, whose feeding and care constitute a problem to the man of the desert. Its possession is an indication of wealth. And now just a little more about the Bedouin's horse, as indeed I know how greatly you are interested. Contrary to the belief of most people, the Arabian horse was a late importation into ancient Arabia. But once there, it had a perfect opportunity to keep its blood pure and free from admixture. As we are all aware, the pure-blooded Arabian horse is known throughout the world for its physical beauty, endurance, intelligence and faithfulness to its master. Yes, the Arabian horse is the origin from which all western ideas about good breeding of horseflesh have been derived."

Alec, vividly recalling the Black's great size and amazing speed, said: "A moment ago you implied that the Bedouin desires to keep the blood of his horses pure and free from admixture. Yet the horse which we're looking for may not be a pure-blooded Arabian. To the best of your knowledge do you think it possible that there might be a Bedouin who is intermingling the blood of Arabian horses with that of other breeds in an effort to create a breed that will have the stamina and heart of the Arabian together with the speed and power of another blood line?"

"Quite possible, Alec," Mr. Coggins replied. "The Bedouin is a past master of horse-breeding, as we all know. Therefore, it's only natural that some of them might attempt to create the perfect horse, especially since the horse's chief value to the Bedouin lies in providing the speed necessary for the success of his raids."

Alec suddenly noticed that Raj had entered the room and was standing silently behind Mr. Volence. He had been listening to the conversation and his soft mouth was tight and grim.

"Are the Bedouins ruthless?" Alec heard Mr. Volence ask.

"No, not unless it's absolutely necessary. In the case of raids no blood is shed except in cases of extreme necessity. The principal causes of conflict are the keen competition for water and good pastures."

Henry moved uneasily in his chair. "Bejabers," he said, "we're sure gonna be lucky if we return in one piece!"

Mr. Coggins said quietly, "On the contrary, Henry, your chances are good. I hope I haven't given you the impression that the Bedouins are inhospitable, because they're not. However dreadful the Bedouin may be to his enemy, he is loyal and generous within the laws of friendship. Hospitality is one of his supreme virtues, and he considers it his sacred duty. He will never refuse a guest, or harm him after accepting him as a guest. It would be an offense against his honor and a sin against God. On the other hand, to make him your enemy is to die. For the law of the desert is that blood calls for blood, and death for death. A blood feud between desert tribes might easily last for fifty years or more.''

Mr. Coggins stopped, glanced at his watch. His gaze shifted to Raj, who nodded. Then he turned to his guests. "A Bedouin is waiting in the other room and I want you to meet him. He may be the guide for you. However, before we go in I want to tell you his story briefly, as it's important that you should be aware of it before you hire him." Mr. Coggins paused a moment before continuing. "This man arrived in Haribwan only a few weeks ago, an outcast from his tribe. He had committed some crime within his clan, escaped with his life, and become an outlaw. The fate of which," he explained, "is worse than death. For to live without protection of a tribe in the desert is in most cases to die many horrible deaths. By some means, however, this Bedouin managed to reach Haribwan alive. His knowledge of the Rub' al Khali is greater than that of any man I've ever met . . . perhaps that accounts for it.

"Knowing that I was looking for a man to guide you across the desert, this man came to my home one night and offered to go. I had seen him in town, and was acquainted with the story I've told you. When I asked him if he didn't fear for his life if he undertook the trip, he didn't answer. He only replied that his fee would be high. He said further that he was one of the few Bedouins of the desert who knew the mountains to the east including the Kharj district. Realizing that I would not be successful in finding another who would take you into the mountains, I told him to return tonight. Now you know the story and it will be up to you to decide. Much thought must be given before you make your decision, for as I have told you, he is an outcast, a man who has lost his tribal affiliation and whose capture means death. Why he chooses to leave Haribwan and take this great risk, I don't know. His fee will be very high, and with the money he may hope to buy his way back into his clan. Anyway, there's no getting around the fact that he is the only man who will take you to the Kharj district. Other guides will go across the desert, but no farther."

Heavy silence fell on the room as Mr. Coggins finished. The faces of Alec, Henry, and Mr. Volence were without expression for they were weighing the risks they would have to take. Raj stood rigidly behind the table.

Finally, Mr. Coggins said, "Your decision does not have to be made at once. Come, and I will show you this Bedouin."

Caravan

7

They entered a long room dimly lighted by one oil lamp which hung like a chandelier from the center of the ceiling. A figure in white rose from the sofa. Slowly he made his way toward them. He stopped only a few yards away and now Alec could distinguish his features which were faintly outlined beneath the white head shawl around which ran a bright red band. With the exception of a deeply furrowed scar that ran from his left ear down to his chin, he was much like the Arabs Alec had seen on the train. He had the same flat cheek bones, broad jaw and straight nose, and like them was of medium height.

For some unexplainable reason, Alec's thoughts suddenly turned to Abu Já Kub ben Ishak, and then to Raj. It was strange that both of them were so unlike the other Arabians he had seen, including Ibn al Khaldun. Raj and Abu Já Kub ben Ishak were tall of stature and high-cheekboned. Alec heard Mr. Coggins' voice as he spoke in Arabic to the newcomer, who bowed slightly, acknowledging the introductions.

"He cannot speak English," Mr. Coggins explained, "so I'll act as interpreter. What are some of the things you'd like to know?"

"See if he can tell us anything about Abu Já Kub ben Ishak . . . where he lives, and if he could guide us to him," Mr. Volence answered.

"Also," said Alec, "if he's ever heard of an Arabian named Ibn al Khaldun."

"Let's not forget," Henry spoke up, "to ask how much this will cost us, and what kind of security he's goin' to give us to make sure he doesn't leave us in the middle of the desert."

Mr. Coggins smiled at Henry's remark. "Yes, that's pretty important," he said. Then, turning to the Arab, he conversed with him.

Soon Mr. Coggins turned back to them. "He's heard of Abu Já Kub ben Ishak," he explained, "but knows nothing about Ibn al Khaldun. Abu Ishak lives in the most mountainous section of the Kharj district. . . . Few have seen him or his home although many in the mountains and the Rub' al Khali know his name."

"Will he attempt to find him for us?" Alec asked.

"Yes, but his fee will be higher. He says the risks involved are great and the compensation must also be great. He asks one thousand dollars."

"A stiff price," Mr. Volence muttered. "Much more than I expected to pay. Will that amount include the cost of the caravan and supplies?"

Mr. Coggins turned to the Arab, spoke with him, then

to Mr. Volence. "Yes, it will include everything. The price, I know, is exorbitant, but we must remember there is no one else who can do the job you want done." He nodded his head in the direction of the Arab. "He knows it, too," he concluded.

Mr. Volence was silent a moment, then asked, "What security will he give?"

"Only his word," Mr. Coggins replied, "but I have yet to regret trusting the word of a Bedouin."

"Even an outcast like him?" Henry questioned.

"Yes, Henry," Mr. Coggins replied. "He may kill and plunder, but his word is good." He turned to Mr. Volence again. "The Bedouin says that only half the fee is necessary now, and from that he will buy supplies and camels and hire the men necessary for the trip. When you return to Haribwan, you will pay him the rest of the money. He cannot assure you that he will find Abu Já Kub ben Ishak, but will continue the search in the mountains until you tell him to return."

Alec watched Mr. Volence closely, awaiting his decision. Would he think it worth the large sum of money asked? They could, he supposed, hire another guide to take them across the desert, but what then? They certainly couldn't seek Abu Já Kub ben Ishak alone. They might attempt to find another guide, but as Mr. Coggins had said, the chances of finding one were very slim and much time would be wasted. Alec felt certain that having gone this far Mr. Volence would not turn back now. He had gambled on many long shots in his life, and would gamble again on finding Abu Já Kub ben Ishak regardless of the high price being asked by the guide.

To the right of Mr. Volence, back in the shadows of the room, Alec saw something move. Looking closer, he distinguished the tall frame of Raj. How long he had been there, Alec did not know. He wanted to know Raj better . . . to find out how he felt about everything—horses, books, school, his life in Arabia. And in turn Alec wanted to tell him about the United States, about his home, about his horse.

Mr. Volence broke the silence. "Tell him, Bruce, that I'll pay his price," he said quietly.

Henry turned to Alec, a broad grin on his face. "I knew he'd come through," he whispered.

Mr. Volence had the gold medallion in his hand. After Mr. Coggins had finished talking with the Arab, Mr. Volence said, "Bruce, ask if this means anything to him."

Mr. Coggins took the medallion and scrutinized it carefully before handing it to the Bedouin. All eyes were turned toward the small man in the white flowing robe. His eyes narrowed as he gazed at it in his hand. Minutes passed and still he did not answer. Alec might have been mistaken in the dim light, but he thought he saw the long muscular fingers tighten over the medallion, then relax.

The Bedouin nodded his head negatively and then handed the medallion back to Mr. Volence. A few minutes later he made his departure after telling them that they should be ready to leave in two days.

After the door had closed behind the Bedouin, Mr. Coggins asked, "This medallion . . . where did you get it?"

Mr. Volence told him the complete story, then asked, "Do you think, Bruce, that it could be the Phoenix?"

"It could have been meant as such, Charlie." Mr.

Coggins lowered his voice and murmured, "The Phoenix, bird of Araby, is rising again. Its wings are strong."

They looked at him questioningly. "What does that mean?" Alec asked.

"I don't know. Just something I happened to think of. Heard an old Arab who returned with a caravan a few weeks ago quote it. I'm surprised I remembered it. Just the association with this," he added, handing the medallion back to Mr. Volence.

The following day was spent in acquiring clothes for the trip. "That's all you have to worry about," Mr. Coggins had told them. "The Bedouin will take care of everything else."

When they returned after having done their shopping, Alec, anxious to see himself in this new raiment, rushed to his room. Carefully he placed the white flowing robe and head shawl on the bed.

When he had finished dressing he stood before a long mirror. Curiously he gazed at his reflection. The head shawl, held tight by a black cord, fell low over his forehead, covering his red hair, and down the back of his neck. A white upper garment was draped loosely over his shoulders, and his legs were covered by a long white skirt held securely by a black sash. His American shoes had been discarded and he wore Bedouin sandals. With freckled face, tanned by the hot Arabian sun, he could have been mistaken for a Bedouin youth, providing one did not approach close enough to see the light-blue eyes and pug nose.

Later that afternoon he walked into the library to find Mr. Volence with their host. They stopped talking as soon as they were aware of Alec's presence. Mr. Coggins held a pistol lightly in his hand. "I was suggesting to Charlie," he told Alec, "that I supply you each with a gun for your own personal use. The Bedouin will secure arms, but it will be better if you have a gun of your own as well."

Mr. Volence looked skeptically at Alec. "Know how to handle one, Alec?"

"Sure. Dad's best friend is a cop in New York, and he used to take us to their indoor pistol range quite often. They said I was a pretty good shot."

"Fine." Mr. Coggins smiled. "I'll have a gun ready for each of you." He turned to Mr. Volence. "Charlie, there's another matter I'd like to talk to you about. The Bedouin, as you know, does not speak any English, and none of you can speak Arabic. Also, chances are that of the few men hired to make the trip, none will speak English."

"I'd thought about that, Bruce. It's had me a little worried. Perhaps we should tell the Bedouin to be sure to hire one man who can speak English."

"I hesitate to do that, Charlie, because he'll hire men best suited for their jobs and may not be able to find a competent man who can also speak English. Furthermore, it would put my mind more at ease if I were certain you had someone you could definitely trust on this trip." He paused, then continued, "I was thinking that Raj might go along with you."

Alec's eyes lighted. It would be great to have someone his own age, with them. "That sounds good," he told them.

"But, Bruce, don't you need him around here?" Mr. Volence asked.

"I'll manage to get along without him for a while," assured their host with a smile. Then his voice became earnest. "Seriously, Charlie, it will be a good change for him. He's never been away from Haribwan, and I'm certain he'd like to make the trip. He's a Bedouin, remember . . . the desert is part of him. I've found him gazing across the Rub' al Khali very often, and he never fails to be on hand to meet an incoming caravan."

Mr. Volence looked at Alec. Raj would no doubt prove to be a great asset on the trip, and he would also be good company for Alec. The boy's eyes were intent. He was waiting for Mr. Volence to make a decision, a favorable one it would seem, from the expression on his eager face.

"Bruce," said Mr. Volence finally, "we'd like very much to have Raj come along."

"Good." Mr. Coggins smiled as he rang a small bell. "Let's tell him."

The door opened and Raj slid silently inside. His head was bare and his heavy black hair was neatly brushed back.

"Raj," Mr. Coggins began, "you know that our guests leave tomorrow for a trip across the Rub' al Khali. We thought you'd like to go with them."

The Bedouin youth was silent for a moment, only his eyes disclosing any emotion. They were wide and full and soft. "I thank you," he said slowly. "I thank you very much."

The caravan was forming on the outskirts of Haribwan. It was to be a large one and their small unit of ten camels was to be a part of it for half the distance across the Rub' al Khali. Then, while the rest of the caravan journeyed on to a great port on the Persian Gulf, they would turn to the south and east.

Dawn was just breaking over the eastern desert when they arrived with Mr. Coggins. It was cold and Alec pulled his shawl of camel's hair tightly about him. There was little confusion and it was obvious from the heavy packs roped securely around the backs of the camels that many hours of work had been done before they arrived. The camels were resting on their knees, heavy mouths working ponderously over their food.

"Gosh, what a mob of 'em!" Henry exclaimed.

"The Bedouin told me it would be a caravan of about five hundred camels," Mr. Coggins said. "One of the biggest . . . which means you'll have little trouble while you're with them."

They threaded their way through the horde of beasts and men. The Bedouins were separated in what seemed to be hundreds of small groups. Mr. Coggins led them toward the rear of the long line, where they found their guide. He walked up to them, nodded, and spoke to Mr. Coggins.

Raj, standing beside Alec, told him, "He says all is ready and soon we will be leaving."

Alec glanced at Henry and Mr. Volence clothed in their white garments. How strange they looked—but no different from him. His gaze swept over his own clothes down to the light sandals on his feet. He raised his hand and pulled the cord on his head shawl farther down. Digging in his deep pocket, he felt the cold steel of the pistol Mr. Coggins had given him.

A cry was heard up front and gradually it swept toward them like an incoming wave. The groups had dispersed and men were walking quickly toward their camels.

Alec felt Raj's hand on his arm. "The Karwan Bashi, leader of the caravan, has given notice to make ready to go," he said.

After bidding Mr. Coggins good-bye and thanking him for all he had done, Alec, Raj, Henry and Mr. Volence made their way to the camels assigned them by the Bedouin guide.

"I'll be seeing you in a couple of months," Mr. Coggins called. "Much luck!" His gaze turned to Raj. "Have fun, boy, and give them all the help you can."

Alec walked up to his camel, which was still kneeling on the ground. One of the men hired by their guide stood at his head. He motioned Alec to mount. Cautiously Alec threw a leg over the back of the camel and sat on the saddle, which was nothing but a heavy piece of cloth covering the single hump. His backrest, however, was made of leather and Alec leaned against it. There were no stirrups, so he gripped the sides of the camel tightly with his knees. Looking back, he saw that the others had also mounted, and that the Bedouins were patiently awaiting the signal to leave.

Another shout rang out and the camels ahead began climbing to their feet. Raj, astride the camel ahead, looked back at Alec and waved.

Seeking support as he felt his camel gather himself, Alec grabbed the forepart of the hump. There was a sudden lurch, frontwards then backwards, and the camel was on his feet. The dark-skinned Bedouin in front smiled, and handed Alec the rope, which was attached to the camel's leather halter. He moved his head, indicating that all Alec had to do was to follow the other camels, then he left.

The sun had risen above the horizon of the Rub' al Khali and its rays were already warm. Their Bedouin guide, riding in front of Raj, was looking impatiently up the line. It was obvious that he wanted to proceed while it was still cool. Behind Alec rode Mr. Volence and then came Henry followed by the rest of their small unit consisting of two Bedouins and three camels heavily laden with baggage and supplies.

The camels ahead were moving. Their guide looked back and waved his arm. Raj moved, swaying back and forth in his saddle. Alec looked at the long crop in his hand and wondered whether it would be necessary to use it. Then he felt a sudden lurch as his camel began jogging slowly to catch up with the others. It was a pacing motion, the camel lifting both feet on the same side successively, and was not uncomfortable. Alec sat easily in the saddle and relaxed.

The single line of camels and Bedouins stretched far into the desert. To the rear was Haribwan. How long before they would return? What lay ahead? Alec's hands tightened over the rope and crop. The final and most important phase in their search for the Black had begun. The sun rose higher on the horizon and Alec removed his warm shawl.

Ships of the Desert

8

The caravan moved at a steady and uniform pace throughout the day, stopping only once during the terrific heat of the afternoon to give them time to eat a light meal of dates and goat's milk. "We'll reach our first oasis before nightfall," Raj told them.

The hot sun beat down unmercifully upon them as they traveled across the endless miles of white sand. Occasionally they would see a cloud of sand in the distance and bounding shapes. *"Ghazlán . . . gazelles,"* Raj would call back to Alec, pointing toward them. "They travel quickly from oasis to oasis," he explained.

Monotonously the hours passed, the camels' padded feet moving tirelessly over the hot sand, the bodies of their riders swaying rhythmically back and forth with the elongated curved necks of the camels.

The sun was low in the west when Raj pointed ahead and said, "*Wâha* . . . oasis."

Alec could see the tops of the date palms rising above the horizon. Those at the head of the caravan would be there in a short time. The pace quickened, and Alec looked back at Mr. Volence and Henry and grinned. It had been a tiring first day. . . . They would sleep well that night.

The following days were repetitious of the first . . . miles and miles of scorching white sand under hot, cloudless skies. Their skin was burned black from the constant blistering sun and glare. Their eyes were barely slits, kept closed most of the time. They seldom spoke to one another during the day and it was only during the cold nights that they were awakened from their trance-like states and looked beyond to the time when the desert would be behind them.

During the evening of the sixth day, after they had eaten a meal of dates and camel flesh, washed down with a beverage made from fermented dates, Raj said, "Our guide informs me that we separate from the others tomorrow morning. Now we are to proceed to the south and east."

Mr. Volence said gravely, "So it's tomorrow."

They were silent, realizing that no longer would they have the protection and security of the large caravan.

"How much longer?" Alec asked Raj, and his voice was tired.

"Only seven more days," he replied. "We can travel faster now."

"Only?" Henry grunted. "Seven more days . . ."

Raj was sympathetic. "I think you'll find the days to come easier," he said.

A little later Alec was left alone, Mr. Volence and Henry having retired to their tent for the night. Raj was tending his camel, which had been limping toward the last part of the day's journey. The sun had gone down and only a red glow in the west kept the day alive. A short distance away Alec saw their Bedouin guide sitting alone, gazing out across the desert to the south. He was always alone, for even the men whom he had hired did not associate with him once the day's work was done. A Bedouin without a tribe, an outcast, and unwanted. What strange thoughts did he think? Did he not fear for his life? Alec supposed so, but it was not obvious from the man's cold countenance.

The red glow in the west flickered and then died. A cold wind swept across the desert. Alec reached for his shawl, and pulled it about him. Then he walked over to Raj, who was anxiously bent over his camel.

"Is he all right?" Alec asked.

"$\hat{E}$ . . . yes. Just a thorn, which I have removed. He will be well tomorrow."

For a minute Alec watched as the camel chewed cakes of crushed date stones, which were his daily food. It was a homely, but friendly face. The sensitive nostrils were oblique, enabling him to close them at will and preventing the entrance of dust and sand. His brown eyes were protected from the glaring sun and drifting sand by long eyelashes. Alec thought how well nature had provided for this "ship of the desert." And rightly so. For without him the desert could not have been conceived of as a habitable place. Alec smiled, for even with the camel it was a difficult enough place in which to live.

"Raj, how long can a camel go without water?" he asked as they walked back toward the tent.

"From three to six days," Raj replied, and then added hesitatingly ". . . Alec."

It was the first time he had called him by his first name, and Alec was glad for he felt that Raj, sensitive and retiring from the beginning of the trip, had finally become a friend with whom he could share many things.

"But how does he do it, Raj?"

The Bedouin youth smiled. "No one knows exactly how he does it. Camels drink a great deal of water when it is available and can make it last a long time."

They had reached the tent and Alec suddenly realized he was very tired. A cold wind swept across his face, but he scarcely felt it, his skin was so toughened by the sun. "Guess I'll go to bed," he said. "I'm pretty sleepy."

Raj smiled. "I will also go soon. Tomorrow there will be much to do, for we will be alone."

The next morning, shivering and cold in the predawn stillness, they stood watching the first of the caravan leave the oasis and head northeast. Before the last of the camels had left they, too, were ready to depart. Alec, astride his camel, waited patiently for their Bedouin guide to give them the signal to start. He glanced back at Henry, Mr. Volence, and the pack camels. All were ready. Riding up the line, the guide passed Alec without a glance. His face was set and the long scar was red against his black skin. When he reached Raj he stopped, spoke to the boy, and then looked back, a grim smile on his lips. He raised his hand, then his crop fell on the flank of his camel.

Taking advantage of the sunless sky, the Bedouin drove the small unit relentlessly to the south and east. The large caravan was soon out of sight in the early morning light. Alec, sitting easily in his saddle, enjoyed the quickened pace and freer movement of the small compact unit. He looked to the east. Dawn was breaking and soon the scorching sun would rise in the heavens. For some reason he did not fear it today as he had in days past. Perhaps he was becoming hardened to desert life. Or perhaps it was the swift freedom of movement.

The Bedouin slackened their pace in the early afternoon. They stopped only once for a light, hasty meal and then went on. Night fell, and they camped in the desert. "When the sun sets tomorrow we shall arrive at another oasis," Raj explained after speaking to the Bedouin guide.

Three days passed without mishap. The Bedouin still drove them forward, stopping only when his keen eyes discovered fresh camel tracks in the sand. Then he would dismount and closely scrutinize them. Usually, after reading the tracks, he would proceed without changing their course. But twice they turned, headed north for hours, then swung once again to the east, their guide's eyes ever on the horizon. Whenever they saw a cloud of sand, he would call a halt until he was satisfied that it was made by gazelles or ostriches. At night he and his men would stand guard, their eyes and ears always alert for any strange sound.

Late on the afternoon of the fourth day, the Bedouin

guide raised his hand and the small caravan came to an abrupt halt. Alec surveyed the horizon in every direction and saw nothing. The Bedouin had dismounted. Quickly he walked a short distance in the sand, and fell to his knees. After a time he rose and with narrowed eyes looked to the east. His face was tense when he returned, mounted his camel, and again started. The pace was slow, nothing more than a fast walk.

The Bedouin led them only a short distance to a deep wadi, which concealed them from all sides. He stopped and signaled to make camp. Alec's gaze turned to the sun. Strange, there was still an hour's good traveling time left in the day.

After pitching their tents and bedding down the camels, they were ready for dinner. Their guide, who had walked to the top of the wadi, returned and talked to Raj. Nodding, Raj made his way toward them. He spoke to Mr. Volence. "He says there is to be no fire tonight. We must eat cold food."

"Any trouble?" Henry inquired.

Raj shook his head. "He did not say, but I suspect there is danger."

They ate in silence. The night before had been spent on an oasis, and their fruit and water were fresh. "One thing to be thankful for," Henry muttered, breaking the silence.

Alec watched the Bedouins who sat apart from their guide. They ate little, their eyes sweeping nervously around the wadi, and then up to the sky, which was strangely overcast in the south.

"Perhaps there's a storm brewing," Alec suggested.

"I feel that it's more than that," Mr. Volence replied. "We might as well try to get some sleep, anyway. There's not much we can do."

Physically spent from the day's hard ride, they slept soundly in spite of the tension. Alec was the first to awaken. Sleepily his gaze turned to the top of the tent, which was shaking. The wind whistled through the flaps. A storm! He shook his head to rouse himself. They would have to make sure the tent poles were secure!

He awakened the others, and hurriedly they pulled on their clothes and left the tent. Outside they felt the strong surge of the gale; blowing sand peppered their faces.

"Afraid it's gonna get worse," Henry yelled, pointing to the blackened sky to the south from which the wind was blowing. To the east only a few stars shone in the ever lightening sky, for dawn was not long off.

The camels were on their feet, moving uneasily and testing the strength of the stakes and ropes to which they were secured.

Alec saw the two Bedouins quickly taking down their tent. "We'd better do the same," he yelled. He looked around for their guide, but could not see him. His tent was still up. "Raj," Alec called to his friend. "Get our guide. Maybe he's sleeping . . ." Strange, he thought, as he helped pull up the tent pegs, that the Bedouin shouldn't be up. It wasn't like him. Then again, he usually had the watch just before dawn.

The wind grew stronger as they folded the tent and quickly tied it to the back of one of the camels. Raj was not back, and their guide's tent was still up! Yelling to the others to follow, Alec ran toward the pitched tent. He met Raj on his way back. "The guide's not there!" Raj yelled.

"He's got to be!" Alec raised his voice above the gale. "Where else . . ."

The others, including the two Bedouins, joined them.

"Raj! Ask them who had the last watch," Alec shouted.

The Bedouins answered, their frantic eyes sweeping from the sky to the pitched tent. "They say the guide had the last watch," Raj said. "He should be here . . . or maybe on top of the wadi," he suggested.

The group started across the depression, but had gone only a short distance when Henry stumbled and fell. Alec, helping him to his feet, saw a still figure half-covered by sand.

"Look!" Alec shouted to the others.

Hands reached down, dragging the white-robed body from the clutching sand. It was the Bedouin guide, his face rigid and still in death. Deep in his chest was the silver hilt of a dagger.

The wind whistled down through the hollow of the wadi, sand covering their intent faces. Alec looked at the others, all of whom realized the gravity of their situation. They were without a guide and the sand storm was getting worse. The two Bedouins exchanged hasty, frightened glances. It was obvious to Alec that they, too, were apprehensive . . . perhaps more so, for they were Bedouins who had associated willingly with an outcast. And where death had struck once it could strike again. The Bedouin had paid for his crime, but death might also be waiting for others, especially those of his own race. The Bedouins had good cause to fear, and so, thought Alec, had he and his friends.

Sand swirled about them. "We must leave him and seek cover," Mr. Volence cried.

They could see only a few feet in front of them as they made their way back toward the camels. Alec, Raj, Henry and Mr. Volence clung together. The two Bedouins had disappeared in the flying sand and dust. After a time they came upon one of their camels, which was lying down. "Get behind him for protection," Raj shouted. "Cover heads with shawls!"

They lay there for a long time, while the wind whistled above their heads and sand covered their bodies. The weight of sand became heavier and heavier, gradually shutting out the sound of the wind above.

The first indication that the storm was over came when the camel moved his great body. Slowly he rose to his knees. Alec also climbed to his feet and the sand poured off him. He threw the shawl from his head and looked around. Skies were blue overhead and the sun shone brightly. Only the dark mass of clouds to the north and the shaking camel in front of him were evidence of the passing storm. The three piles of sand beside him stirred and Henry, Raj and Mr. Volence emerged, shaking themselves vigorously.

The Bedouins and the other camels were nowhere to be seen.

"Where could they be?" Mr. Volence asked anxiously.

"Probably buried," Henry offered.

"*La* . . . no," Raj said, "the camels would not let the sand bury them. They have gone." He paused, then added slowly, "They have deserted us . . ."

"No!" Mr. Volence exclaimed. "They wouldn't . . . they couldn't do that to us at a time like this. They must be in the sand. Hurry, let's try to find them before it's too late!"

They ran toward the place where they had last seen the camels. Raj, jogging beside Alec, shook his head. "No, Alec . . . Mr. Volence is wrong . . . they have deserted us. They feared the same fate as that which befell the guide even more than they feared the storm. Not wanting to go with us any farther, they have gone and have taken the camels and our supplies with them."

They searched in vain. Nothing was found. Raj was right. . . . They had been left alone, without food, without water . . . to die.

Desert Raiders

9

They stood in the wadi, silent and alone. The camel beside them rested on his knees, waiting patiently until he was made to move.

"Well, what now?" Henry asked.

"Let's think for a few minutes," Mr. Volence said, his voice grave.

"There's a canteen half full of water," Alec said. He had found it in the sand. "It'll last a while if we use it sparingly."

"Nothing else?"

"No," Raj answered. "Our provisions were all packed on the camels." He paused, then continued. "I suggest that we continue to the south and east for we were but three days' distance from the mountains yesterday."

"Yes, Raj, I suppose you're right," Mr. Volence

agreed. "But there's no telling how long it will take us on foot, and with no food and so little water . . ."

Henry jerked his head toward the camel. "Two of us can ride him at one time," he said, "and we can take turns. That'll help."

"We have our guns," Alec offered. "We can hunt . . . there are gazelles."

Nodding, Mr. Volence turned to the Bedouin youth. "Raj," he said, "lead the way . . . we're pretty much in your hands."

All that day they walked, stumbling through the burning sand. They took turns riding the camel, Alec and Henry changing with Raj and Mr. Volence every hour. They had done nothing more than wet their lips with water. For when that was gone . . .

Alec searched the desert constantly for the sight of some living thing. Gazelles . . . ostriches . . . Bedouins; yes, even the ones who had killed their guide. Anything . . . anyone.

The sun set, but they kept on until the heavy desert night fell upon them. Then, exhausted, they lay down beside the camel and slept.

Raj awakened them before dawn. "Come," he said, "let us go before the sun rises."

Silently they rose, and in a few minutes were once again on their way, trusting Raj to lead them in the right direction.

Late that afternoon they stopped to rest. Hunger gnawed their vitals; faces were gaunt and thin; throats were parched and tight, making it an effort to speak above a hoarse whisper.

Alec raised his glassy, bloodshot eyes to the canteen in Raj's hand. He shook it and held it to his ear; then, without drinking, he passed it on to Henry, who raised it to his lips. A swallow, and it was passed on to Mr. Volence; then to Alec. He shook it, and there was just the slight swish of water inside. He wet his lips and gave it to Raj. "Finish it," he said, and only the words formed on his lips; there was no sound.

They moved on. No water, no food. What was the use? Alec walked behind the camel. They could kill it, he thought, and they would have to before long. They could go another day without food, perhaps, but water . . . Alec pressed his hand against his throat.

That night Raj crawled over to Alec as Henry and Mr. Volence slept. Shaking his friend, he called him. Alec's eyes opened. "I need your help. Come," Raj said.

Raj led Alec to the camel. "We must tie his feet," the Bedouin youth explained, two pieces of rope in his hand. Alec wondered why, but nodded in agreement, his heavy, thick tongue making it impossible to ask questions.

Laboriously they tied the camel's fore and hind legs, then Raj reached for his thick crop and a piece of canvas which had been part of the saddle. He handed Alec the canvas and then grasped the camel's head halter. With skilled hands he quickly pried open the camel's mouth and shoved the crop down his throat, calling to Alec at the same time to hold the canvas underneath.

The camel bellowed, heaved, then vomited water from the chambers in his stomach. Alec caught the precious liquid in the canvas. Together he and Raj poured it into the canteen, untied the camel's legs, and without further conversation lay down to sleep, the canteen between them.

The next day was worse than the others. Tired legs faltered and crumpled under the weight of thin, starved bodies. The liquid in the canteen was wet, tolerable. But stomachs cried for food, and crazed eyes lingered longingly on the camel. "We will kill it tonight," Raj whispered hoarsely to Alec. "He is almost done . . . we have his water . . . he is stumbling . . . it is the only way."

Alec nodded, and let his tired, heavy head fall upon his chest.

When the sun went down and darkness came, they put a bullet through the camel's head, and feasted on its flesh. Satisfied, they fell into a heavy sleep.

The next morning they cleaned the camel of its meat, left the carcass for the hyenas and jackals, and strengthened by the food, set out once more.

Mile after mile of sand passed under their feet as the sun rose in the cloudless sky. Alec's eyes swept continuously across the horizon to the southeast, seeking the mountains toward which they were presumably headed. It was the fifth day and soon, if Raj had led them straight on their course, they should come to them. Night fell and still only miles and miles of white sand lay before them.

The next day was the same, and so was the following one. Feet lagged heavily across the sand. Little camel meat was left. The last of the water was gone. Alec fell and Raj helped him to his feet. "Place your arm on my shoulder for a while, Alec," he said. "Let us not stop, for it is best that we keep on."

A little later Mr. Volence fell to his knees, followed by Henry. Alec and Raj stumbled back to them. Their eyes were glazed and swollen tongues protruded between cracked lips. This is the end, Alec thought, the end of everything. Then his mind went blank . . . he was too tired to care much. The sun was setting and a cool breeze swept across the desert from the east. Alec turned his body toward it for it relieved somewhat the dull ache in his head. He struggled to open his eyes, hoping the breeze would cool the fires inside. His vision, dulled by the heat and glare, cleared slowly until he could see. Rising above the horizon was a dark, jagged shape. He blinked his eyes and tried again. It was still there. His gaze swept to the right. It was there, too. Then to the left. And there! Hope surged through his mind and body. They could be the mountains . . . they could be!

Alec turned and touched Raj's shoulder. Feebly he pointed to the east. Raj looked, then rose to his feet. Slowly a smile cracked his blackened lips. He fell to his knees and lifted Henry's and Mr. Volence's faces to the east. "Mountains," he whispered in their ears. "Mountains . . . tomorrow . . . tomorrow."

The cold night descended upon them with Raj's words still ringing in their ears . . . "tomorrow."

It was already light when Alec awoke. He turned his head and saw that the others were still sleeping. Another day and they must get going . . . he stopped as he suddenly remembered. The mountains! This was tomorrow! Or had it been a dream? Were there mountains to the east or had it been just a mirage? Alec struggled to a sitting position.

The sun was not yet fully over the horizon. But the horizon! It was not that of sand meeting sky, as it had been for days and days past. Instead jagged peaks pierced the heavens, pierced the sun. They had been right. It had not been a mirage, not a dream brought on by tired, bewildered minds. Ahead were the mountains. Their destination! Water! Food!

A cry escaped Alec's lips, rousing the others. He pointed a trembling arm to the east.

Late in the afternoon they reached the mountains. An unknown force had provided them with the last bit of energy and strength needed to drag their tired bodies across the last few miles of blistering sand.

A short distance from where the desert ended and the short sun-scorched grass began, they saw a small spring gurgling forth from the rocks. Stumbling, they reeled toward it and lowered their heads into the cool water.

They rested that day and the following one. Dates and other fruit were abundant at the foot of the mountains. Slowly their strength returned; gradually their stomachs stopped crying for food. On the morning of the second day after their arrival Raj and Alec went hunting and brought back a young gazelle which Raj had shot. As they ate their spirits rose. "Gettin' so I feel as though I was always meant for this kinda life," said Henry with a grin, rubbing a sun-blackened hand to wipe his mouth free of food after he had finished eating.

Alec, too, felt well enough to start looking ahead again in their search for the Black. Even though they had been successful in crossing the desert, they still had no guide. Where to now? How could they possibly find Abu Já Kub ben Ishak? In which direction was the Kharj district? Yes, they had reached the mountains, but they were still lost. He turned to Mr. Volence. "What do you think we should do next?" he asked.

Mr. Volence shrugged his shoulders. "Your guess is as good as mine, Alec," he answered. "The Kharj district, from what I've learned, is still far to the northeast, somewhere high in the mountains. It seems to me that it's practically impossible to find it without a guide. What do you think?" he asked, turning to the others.

"Might I suggest," Raj said quietly, "that we proceed north up the mountain range, keeping close to the desert. It is quite possible that we will find a village, where we might be fortunate enough to find someone who can lead us to the Kharj district."

Henry slapped his hand against his knee. "That sounds like a good idea," he said enthusiastically.

The others nodded in agreement.

Early the following morning they departed. Walking in single file, they kept close to the mountains, avoiding the hot sun as much as they possibly could. Their muscles, hardened by the days spent in the desert, made walking on the solid ground easy. Springs and date palms were numerous, and every few hours they would stop to rest.

Two days passed without change. On the morning of the third day Raj, who was leading, raised his hand, signaling them to stop. "*Yashûf* . . . look!" he exclaimed, pointing across the desert to the west.

A cloud of sand was moving rapidly toward them. Forms were now taking shape. Not gazelles . . . not ostriches. Alec strained his eyes. There could be no mistake. A large group of horsemen was riding out of the desert!

"Raiders?" asked Mr. Volence of Raj.

The Bedouin youth shrugged his shoulders. "Perhaps," he said, his eyes never leaving the desert. "They travel fast."

"What are we gonna do?" Henry asked. "Attract their attention or hide till they've gone? They might be the same bunch that knifed our guide!"

Alec reminded them of Mr. Coggins' words, "The Bedouin is loyal and generous within the laws of friendship . . . hospitality is one of his supreme virtues, and he considers it his sacred duty." He suggested that they go out to meet the rapidly approaching group.

"Perhaps you're right, Alec," Mr. Volence said. "We just can't go on hiding out from Bedouins. I'm also in favor of stopping them." He turned to the others and they, too, nodded approval.

The horsemen were only a short distance away and the sound of pounding hoofs in sand could be heard easily. Mr. Volence's party had walked down to the edge of the desert and soon could make out the hard-riding figures. There were about twenty of them, sitting still and straight in their saddles as their steeds moved effortlessly across the sand. Alec grasped Henry by the arm. "Those horses. Look at them, Henry!"

Never in Alec's life had he seen so magnificent a group of horseflesh. Blacks, bays, chestnuts galloped swiftly with heads held high and hot coats shining in the sun. They were very near now and Alec's gaze swept to the chestnut in the lead. He was a stallion, much larger than the others, with flowing golden mane and tail and four white stockings.

"What an animal," Henry muttered.

"He's big, Henry," Alec said softly, "as big as the Black!"

The Bedouins had seen them, and their leader astride the chestnut signaled his band to stop. Then he and one of his men proceeded toward them. His stallion, rebelling against the bit that now held him to a walk, pranced with nervous ankles, eyes wide and staring, nostrils dilated and red. The white-robed figure on his back sat erect and still.

He was tall and big-boned. His smooth face, except for the great black beard, was dark and unlined, his brown eyes gentle. Like Raj he, too, had high cheek bones. It was difficult to guess his age. He was a free young man, a man in the making. Long limbs, wrapped around the chestnut's girth, made the stallion dance as he stood there. A slight smile played upon the chieftain's hard-set mouth as he viewed the group. Then he spoke in Arabic, and his voice was soft.

When he had finished, Raj answered. Then they conversed, their words precise but soft-spoken. How alike they were, Alec thought. The same high forehead and cheekbones, the same brown, liquid-soft eyes and set mouth. They talked for some time. Alec heard Raj mention the name of Abu Já Kub ben Ishak, and saw a heavy scowl fall over the face of the young chieftain. In an instant it was gone.

Finishing, Raj turned to his friends. "I have told him our story," he said, "and he will take us into the mountains."

"To Abu Já Kub ben Ishak's?" Alec asked excitedly. "I heard you mention his name."

"*La* . . . no," replied Raj. "He refuses to take us all the way, but has consented to leave us near enough to the kingdom of Abu Já Kub ben Ishak for us to reach it alone."

Henry grinned. "Say, that's good of him," he bellowed. "I knew they were regular guys when I saw 'em!"

"Think we can trust them?" Mr. Volence asked skeptically.

Raj shrugged his large shoulders. "This is the land of the nomad, sir, where one cannot be certain of anything."

The hoofs of the stallion clattered on the stones as he danced nervously in the sun, his coat shining like bright gold. The Bedouin on his back was eager to be off. He spoke to Raj again and there was a terseness in his speech that had not been there before.

Raj turned to his friends. "He will not wait any longer," he said. "If we are going with him, we must go now."

They followed the chieftain and his aide back to the group of horsemen, who looked at them curiously. Assigned to ride with four of the men, they mounted quickly and were off.

Alec found himself on the back of a dappled gray which, in spite of his double burden, kept up with the others. The Bedouin with whom Alec shared his saddle looked back and grinned.

Soon the desert was behind them and out of sight. The Bedouins slowed their horses down to a trot as they picked their way through narrow gorges. To the east, the direction in which they were headed, the mountains rose higher and higher against the sky.

Hour after hour passed without a stop. They followed no path, but it was obvious to Alec that each horseman had traveled this route many times. Ever upward they went, slowing down to a walk to spare their steeds when the ascent became too abrupt.

Sometime in the afternoon they came to a wide plateau, where they stopped to rest. While the Bedouins were attending their horses, Alec made his way in the direction of the chestnut stallion. If ever there was a horse whose physical perfection and beauty matched the Black's this was it. Loyal to the memory of his horse, Alec hoped, frankly, to find the chestnut lacking in some quality.

The young Bedouin chieftain had removed the saddle from the chestnut stallion. The horse walked forward with his head low, sniffing the ground. Finally, finding a depression, he lowered his large body carefully. Then, swinging over on his back, he swung himself from side to side, kicking his free white-stockinged legs in the air and grunting with pleasure as he drove his back into the ground. Pausing, he lay still, then scrambled to his feet, shook himself, snorted about, his head high and ears cocked.

Alec, sensing someone in back of him, turned and met the flashing eyes of the Bedouin chief. He smiled and nodded his head toward the chestnut.

"Sagr!" the chieftain called, and his horse trotted toward him.

He stopped as he neared Alec and the whites of his eyes showed. His big body trembled and he pawed the ground. The Bedouin moved forward and grabbed him by the gold mane; then he stroked the slender, arched neck and small head, which was so much like the Black's.

The Black and this chestnut. What a match that would

be, thought Alec. And the winner? Alec favored his horse, but only because he knew well the courage and heart that were the Black's.

A short time later they were on their way again. They crossed the plateau at a slow gallop and then assembled in single file as they began a still higher ascent. Ahead, Alec could see towering peaks, and below and behind, the mountainous gutted country through which they had already passed. Still farther to the west he could still see the white desert, over which they would have to pass again before returning to Haribwan.

That night they slept on the side of the high mountain range. Lying on his back, Alec stared at the stars. Later he rolled over on his side and watched the horses silhouetted against the sky. He listened to them cropping the grass and saw their sudden starts. Grazing only a short distance away was the chestnut stallion; beside him lay the young chieftain. Alec suddenly wondered what the man's name was. That was something he doubted they would be able to learn. Finally, Alec's eyes closed and he slept.

All the following morning they continued to climb, reaching the top of the range by noon. Just below them, Alec saw another plateau and ahead more mountains, even higher than those which they had just climbed.

When they reached the plateau the Bedouins kicked their horses into a fast gallop for over a mile, then suddenly they slowed to a walk. Their chieftain signaled with upswept arm and two of his men spurted to the right flank and another pair to the left.

As they cantered forward once more Alec noticed that the Bedouins had unslung their guns and were riding with them across their thighs. This was not peaceful country through which they were riding so quietly, and the men who rode were not traders, but desert-hardened warriors who knew well their work as raiders and hunters.

For two days they advanced over the same kind of country, in the same formation, at the same speed.

One night as they camped Alec turned to Raj; they sat in a small group apart from the Bedouins. "Raj," he asked, "how much longer?"

"I do not know, Alec. The man with whom I am riding will not say."

"Can't be much farther," Henry growled, "we been ridin' four days now. Besides," he continued, nodding toward the mountains which were closing in on them, "we've just about come to the end of this plateau."

Mr. Volence smiled. "We can always go up, Henry," he said.

"Not much . . . or we won't be able to breathe," Henry muttered, sniffing the thin air.

They pressed on again as soon as it was light. After cantering for about a mile the Bedouin chieftain led his band up a steep ravine. They traveled swiftly in spite of the rugged country. Precipitous cliffs on which rose great masses of rock that seemed to totter precariously were on all sides of them. The Bedouins' skilled hands guided their horses as they zigzagged through hazardous trails, rising and falling with the terrain.

All morning and far into the afternoon they continued their ascent until only towering peaks rose above them. As the sun gradually fell behind the mountain range in back of them they came to an abrupt fork in the ravine, and it was there that they camped for the night.

After they had eaten the dried meat which the Bedouins had given them, Alec and his friends sat in silence upon the hard and stony ground. It was unusually quiet that evening. No fires burned and double sentries had been posted.

It was after dark when the tall, white-robed young chieftain came toward them, his black beard pressed deep against his chest. He called Raj to one side, conversed for a minute, and then walked away.

"We are near the kingdom of Abu Já Kub ben Ishak," Raj told them when he returned. "Tomorrow morning we separate."

"In which direction do we go?" Alec asked anxiously.

Raj nodded to the fork northeast of them. "They take the other," he said. "The chieftain says it is only a day's journey by foot. He will give us supplies."

Although physically tired from the day's long climb, Alec could not get to sleep. He could only think of tomorrow. What would it bring? Would Abu Já Kub ben Ishak resent their arrival? Again he recalled Mr. Coggins' words concerning the Bedouin's hospitality: "He will never refuse a guest. It would be an offense against his honor . . . a sin against God." Alec rolled on the hard ground and lay on his side, watching the dark figures of the Bedouins as they slept. Yes, they were generous. They had proved that by accepting Mr. Volence's party and taking them this far. There was no reason to fear them or Abu Já Kub ben Ishak.

But Alec remembered the still, crumpled figure of their guide lying in the sand, the long knife stuck to the hilt in his chest. He recalled how Mr. Coggins had also told them, "To make him your enemy is to die . . . the law of the desert is that blood calls for blood, and death for death."

When dawn broke, Alec had not slept, but he was not tired. His body was eager and tense, filled with energy for the journey ahead. The Black was near . . . another day. He was impatient to be off. Shaking his friends, he awakened them. "Come, it's time to go!"

Later, as they were eating, the Bedouin chieftain came to them. His horses were still unsaddled; he appeared to be in no hurry.

"Raj," Alec said, "tell him we'd like to leave. Ask if we may have food for our journey now." His voice was clipped, excited.

After Raj had finished speaking, the Bedouin chieftain smiled as he replied, his brown eyes on Alec. When he had finished Raj told Alec, "He says you have grown your spurs. It is a good sign to be impatient, and he likes to see it. If we want to go now, we can. The supplies are ready."

They left as the Bedouins were saddling their horses; eyes turned momentarily toward the small group and then swept back to their mounts. The chieftain, having finished saddling Sagr, turned toward them. Alec raised his hand. The Bedouin smiled, mounted, and then pulled the stallion back onto his haunches.

As Alec took up the trail behind the others, he wondered if they would ever meet again.

Home of the Black

10

It was late afternoon when the ravine suddenly narrowed and the walls of stone closed about them. Ahead was only a slender chasm in the rocks. As they neared it they saw that it was just large enough for two men to pass through abreast.

Raj led the way and they walked until they came to an abrupt turn.

"Say," Henry muttered, "this is no place for me with my claustrophobia!"

As they rounded the turn, the cleft in the rocks suddenly ended and they found themselves overlooking a large valley. Trees were numerous and the ground was covered with a luxuriant green grass, the like of which Alec had not seen since they had left home.

"Look!" Alec shouted, pointing to a broad, treeless

expanse in the center of the valley below, where a large band of horses was grazing.

"There must be hundreds of them," Mr. Volence exclaimed. "This must be Abu Já Kub ben Ishak's domain."

"There are buildings farther up the valley," Raj said.

Their eyes swept in the direction of Raj's extended arm. In the far corner of the valley, buildings of white stone reflected the rays of the setting sun. One stood apart from the others and was set back against the towering mountains. The other buildings were smaller and arranged in groups along the side of the valley.

They followed a well-worn path down through the brush, Alec's eyes constantly scanning the band of horses below. Was his horse there?

After a time they came to the floor of the valley. Stopping, they watched the horses grazing a half-mile away. Suddenly one broke away from the others. He ran slowly around the band and then stood still, his nose pointed in the direction of the upper valley.

"Henry!" Alec shouted. "It's the Black. . . . I'm sure it's *he!*"

"May be," Henry replied skeptically. "He's too far away to be certain. Sure moved like him, though."

The horse broke into a gallop, his head held high and mane flying in the wind. Alec watched for a moment, then turned to Henry, who said softly, "It's him, all right, Alec. No doubt about that."

Suddenly, far up the valley toward which the black stallion ran, a white horse and rider appeared. Moving swiftly with giant strides, the Black approached them.

Alec saw him stop a short distance from the white horse, hesitate, then half rear.

"Wonder what he's up to," Henry muttered. "Let's get goin'."

Rapidly they walked up the valley, their eyes on the small group far ahead. Then they stopped, as they saw the white horse and rider bolt forward. The Black followed for a short distance, then with a burst of speed passed the white horse.

They were coming swiftly in Alec's direction, when he saw the rider pull his horse to an abrupt halt. The Black whirled and was on his way back, when suddenly he stopped. Turning, he lifted his nose high in the wind that blew from the south. Tossing his head, he pranced nervously.

"Maybe he's caught our scent," Henry told Alec. Then, smiling, he added, "Betcha the white horse is a filly . . . maybe his girl friend."

The Black was looking in their direction. Then he screamed . . . a long whistle, shrill, loud and clear. He ran a short distance toward them, stopped and reared. Again he came on. Again he stopped and reared. He was close now, only a few hundred yards away, and his black body glistened in the sun.

Suddenly Alec broke from the group and ran toward his horse.

The stallion shook his small, savage head and then trotted up to meet the boy running toward him.

When the rest of the group reached them, Alec had his arm around the long, slender neck of the Black. The stallion's ears swept back as the others approached.

Henry walked up to him. "Hey," he said, grasping the long mane, "that's no way to greet an old friend." Turning to Alec, he added, "Looks mighty good, Alec . . . better than I've ever seen him."

The sound of running hoofs made them turn. Coming toward them was the white horse, and their gaze turned to the slim, hatless rider on its back.

"Looks like a kid," Henry commented.

"Wearing European clothes," Mr. Volence pointed out.

A few minutes later, the rider slowed his horse down to a walk and came cautiously toward them.

Henry's eyes were on the horse. It was a pure-blooded Arabian, no doubt about that. Small . . . not over fourteen hands . . . but beautifully proportioned. And a filly, as he had guessed. Her neck rose to a crest like the Black's and she had the same small head, but not the savageness. She walked quietly toward them; devoted to her rider, she had complete confidence in the hands guiding her reins. Henry knew there were few horses like her to be found in the world. He looked at the rider and his eyes narrowed. The figure was slim . . . yes, like a kid's . . . but that of a girl in her late teens!

It was obvious to all of them as horse and rider came to a stop. Her skin was honey-colored; sleek-oiled hair crowned a heart-shaped face, and oblique almond eyes peered curiously at them. She was neither white nor black, neither of the East nor of the West. Her full lips parted and she spoke in Arabic, her voice low and husky.

Raj answered her.

When he had finished, she turned to the others and said softly in English, "Welcome to the home of Abu Já Kub ben Ishak. I am his daughter, Tabari."

They introduced themselves, and then she turned to Alec, who was rubbing the thin-skinned, pink muzzle of the Black. "It is a great surprise and joy to meet you, Alec Ramsay. My father has told me of you and Shê-tân," she smiled. "We are very grateful."

"Your father . . . is he here?" Mr. Volence inquired.

"Yes. Come, and I will take you to him."

As they walked up the valley, Alec looked longingly at the Black, who kept near him. It would be so easy to mount and ride. He had waited so long for this day. He glanced at Tabari, and found her looking at him. As though knowing what was in his mind, she said, "It is better to wait. My father allows only one man to ride Shêtân." Smiling, she added, "Perhaps he will make an exception. . . ."

They reached the band of horses, who raised their heads from their grazing and moved slowly to the south at sight of the Black. Bolting away from Alec, the stallion encircled the horses, his black mane flowing like wind-swept flame.

"These horses . . ." Mr. Volence spoke to the girl, "I have never seen any like them."

"There aren't any others like them," she answered softly. "My father and his father before him have spent their lives interbreeding the original Nejdi purebread strain, like my Jôhar"—she stroked the long neck of her horse—"with others which they have sought throughout the Middle East. These horses are the result, and Shêtân is the finest of them all."

They had almost reached the upper end of the valley when she spoke to Raj. "This chieftain you told me about, the one who brought you here . . . did he make known his name?"

Raj shook his head.

The girl was silent for a moment, then asked, "He was young, was he not? And riding a chestnut stallion?"

"It was difficult to tell his age," Raj replied. "Yes, he rode a chestnut stallion."

No further questions were asked by the girl, and it seemed to Alec that she suddenly withdrew from them. She rode in silence, her eyes on the mountains ahead.

They passed the small white homes, in front of which men and women watched curiously as they walked by. "It is not often that they see strangers," Tabari explained.

As they approached the home of Abu Já Kub ben Ishak, they heard the pounding of hoofs and, turning, saw the Black running toward them. He stopped a short distance away and reared, his forelegs pawing the air. Then he trotted up to Alec.

"Looks as though he's still your horse, Alec," Henry said.

Abu Já Kub ben Ishak was standing on the steps of his home when they arrived. He wore the white flowing gown of the Bedouin, but his steel-gray head was uncovered. His black eyes swept curiously from one to another until finally they came to rest upon Alec. Slowly a look of amazement appeared on his face.

"*Âfferin!* Are *you* Alec Ramsay?" he asked incredulously.

"Sure am, sir," Alec replied, "and you remember

Henry Dailey . . .'' He stopped and his gaze shifted to Mr. Volence. Suddenly he realized how they had all changed, why it had been difficult for Abu Já Kub ben Ishak to recognize him. Their skin was as black as any Bedouin's, and their eyes burned deep in dark sockets. Their faces were haggard and drawn. It would have been difficult for even their best friends to have recognized them let alone Abu Já Kub ben Ishak, who had met them only once.

Alec heard Abu Já Kub ben Ishak say, "Certainly. I remember Henry. I must say that it's all rather incredible . . . your being here, I mean . . . difficult to believe. But come inside . . . You must be tired. I'll have hot baths drawn for you . . . Later we will talk.''

He led the way into the house. Before following the others, Alec turned to the Black. "See you later, fella.'' The stallion snorted and pushed Alec with his head. Then he whirled and ran toward his band.

Later that evening, after they had bathed and changed into clean white gowns provided by Abu Ishak, they told him their story of the trip from Haribwan. Their Bedouin host listened intently, and only when they told him of the young chieftain who had guided them through the mountains did his countenance change, a sullen look falling over his mahogany-colored face and his eyes clouding. He interrupted Mr. Volence, who had been talking, and said slowly, his short white beard jutting out as he spoke, "A difficult time . . . a very difficult time. You are fortunate to be here. But now let us eat, as you must be very hungry.''

They entered a large chamber in the center of which

was a long rectangular table laden with food and great varieties of fruit in silver vessels studded with gems. Three Bedouin servants glided silently around the room, their footsteps making no sounds on the thick, luxurious rugs.

During dinner, Alec heard Mr. Volence say to their host, "As we came through the valley today, we saw your horses. Never have I seen any to equal them. Thoroughbred-breeding is my business," he explained.

Abu Já Kub ben Ishak smiled. "It is the life of the Bedouin," he said quietly. "The horses you saw today are the result of generations of breeding. There are none finer in the world."

Mr. Volence was silent for a few minutes. Then he said, "The black stallion . . . your Shêtân. Would you sell him? I'm willing to pay almost anything you ask."

Without looking at Mr. Volence, Abu Já Kub ben Ishak replied, "He is not for sale." His black eyes lifted and met those of Mr. Volence. "He is above the price of money."

"And the others," Mr. Volence asked, "would you sell any of them?"

After a few seconds of silence, Abu Já Kub ben Ishak answered, "We are very proud and jealous of our horses, Mr. Volence. In the desert there may be a shortage of food, of water, and our children may cry from thirst and hunger; but we give our horse the last drop of water, the last morsel of food." He paused, then continued, "We do not sell our horses. Their blood is pure and free from admixture, except in instances where we think that our line will be improved by careful interbreeding with other strains. Such as I have done," he added, "and my father, and his father before him."

"Yet," Mr. Volence interrupted, "the blood of Arabians flows in many of our horses, including some of mine. I have seen several Arabians back home and in England. If, as you say, you and your people do not sell your horses, where did they come from?"

Abu Já Kub ben Ishak straightened in his chair and shrugged his shoulders. "I think, in fact I am certain, Mr. Volence, that you have seen only one Arabian of purest blood, and that was Jôhar, the white one my daughter, Tabari, was riding today. There are few others like her in Arabia, and certainly none in any foreign country."

They finished dinner in silence.

Alec walked beside Tabari as they left the large chamber. Behind him he heard Mr. Volence say quietly to Abu Já Kub ben Ishak, "I apologize for anything I have said which may have offended you. It was only because I am so very much interested in improving the bloodline of the American thoroughbred that I wanted to buy your horses. I understand now why you won't sell. . . ."

Tabari led Alec out the door onto the porch. Moonlight illuminated the valley, and Alec could see the horses as they moved slowly in their grazing. The sound of voices and music drifted toward them from the homes of the Bedouins.

Tabari's slim body was covered with a single garment of pale-pink silk. Leaning against one of the white stone pillars, she turned her head and said, "Do not let my father's words discourage you. He is a kind and generous man."

"You mean . . . you think he'll sell some of his horses to Mr. Volence?" Alec inquired anxiously.

"No. You see, he meant it when he said our people do not sell their horses." Noticing the depressed look which clouded Alec's face, she smiled and added, "He may give them to you, though. My father is like that." She paused and then said in a lower key, which was barely audible, "So much depends upon Shêtân . . ."

"Shêtân . . . the Black? Why?" Alec asked.

She did not answer him immediately. Then, "It is a strange story, but one that you have a right to know, as you have played a part in it."

"I?" interrupted Alec. "I . . . I played a part in it?"

Tabari nodded, then continued. "But I will start at the beginning. More than one hundred years ago my great-great-grandfather bred a horse which he thought the finest in Arabia, and he made his claim known far and wide. Many chieftains accepted his challenge and a race was run."

"Did he win?" Alec broke in impatiently.

"Yes, he won. And fifteen of the finest horses from each of the tribes entering the race were given to him, for they had agreed upon such stakes before the race. Since that day similar races have taken place every five years; the years in between are spent by the chieftains in breeding the finest possible horses.

"The years passed and the races continued. My great-grandfather bred horses for the express purpose of winning these races after his father died. My father's father carried on, and now my father. When he dies, my brother, who is now studying in England, and I will continue."

"Has your family won all of these races throughout the years? Alec asked.

"No, but we won most of them until twenty years ago, when my father's great bay, Tigris, was beaten by the horse of Abd-al-Rahman. And his horses have also won the two races which have been run since that time."

Tabari raised her eyes to Alec, looked at him questioningly for a minute, then continued. "Perhaps it is best that I tell you more concerning Abd-al-Rahman . . . and his son, the young Bedouin chieftain who guided you through the mountains, and who bears his name."

"Then the chestnut stallion he was riding," Alec interrupted, "will be in the race?"

The girl nodded.

Alec's head whirled. What a race that would be! Just wait until he told Henry. Never would there be one to equal it. Tabari's voice penetrated his thoughts and he turned to her again.

"Perhaps you noticed how my father did not encourage you to talk about him. The feeling is bitter between them . . . at times so bitter that much blood has been shed. It is not because my father has lost to Abd-al-Rahman's horses," she hastened to assure him, "but because of Abd-al-Rahman's intense hatred of my father."

"But why should he hate a kind man like your father?" Alec asked.

Tabari's voice was low and unsteady when she answered. "Twenty years ago his father and mine were the best of friends. They and their tribesmen rode together both in the mountains and in the desert, providing good grazing land and helping those in need who could not provide for themselves. Then one day soon after Abd-al-Rahman's second son was born, he set out on a pilgrimage across the desert to Mecca. With him he took his wife and newborn babe. My father advised him against it, for tribal wars were many at that time, and even a well-known and powerful sheikh such as Abd-al-Rahman was in danger. He would not listen for he was proud of his sword, his men, his horses. Abd-al-Rahman departed, taking with him his best and most loyal men, and leaving behind his two-year-old son."

Tabari stopped and was silent for such a length of time that Alec thought she had finished her story. He was about to speak, when without looking at him, she said, "They were never seen alive again. The bodies of Abd-al-Rahman and his wife and men were found in the desert, rotted by the sun. Only the body of the newborn babe was not there."

The girl's voice faltered as she continued. "In the heart of Abd-al-Rahman they found my father's knife . . . and they brought it back to the young son of Abd-al-Rahman, who bore his name. And it was that upon which he was weaned until hatred for my father coursed through every vein in his body. As he grew older and became strong in mind and body, the red blood of hate surged until very often it took with it the blood of my people.

"When young Abd-al-Rahman was old enough to understand, my father attempted to explain to him that he would not kill his best friend. Failing, he withdrew and when members of our tribe were killed by those of young Abd-al-Rahman, he knew only one law . . . that which reads: *Blood calls for Blood!"*

Tabari raised her oblique eyes until they met those of Alec. "The blood feud between our families will continue until one of us is no more."

Alec was silent when she had finished. His gaze swept over the moonlit valley to the mountains beyond. That, then, explained why the men of Abd-al-Rahman had proceeded with such caution when they neared the valley of Abu Já Kub ben Ishak . . . why they had unslung their guns, riding with them across their thighs. He turned back to the girl. "The race," he said quietly, "isn't very important when you're at war, is it?"

"But it is," she replied huskily, "for to the Arab the horse is responsible for the success of his raids. To lose these races is to lose horses, which in turn weakens a tribe. Through the years my family has become strong and powerful by winning races and acquiring the horses of other tribes. Now Abd-al-Rahman grows powerful, for in winning the last three races he has taken many of my father's best horses. If he wins this year, his tribe will be more powerful than ever before, and it is the feeling of my father that with his new strength he will seek the revenge that has long enveloped his heart."

Tabari moved from the pillar against which she had been leaning, and turned her back to Alec. "You can understand now why so much depends upon Shêtân's winning this race. When he was stolen my father suspected Abd-al-Rahman and descended upon him with his strongest and bravest men. Much blood would have been shed had not word reached my father before he arrived at the domain of Abd-al-Rahman that Bedouins leading a horse of Shêtân's description had been seen crossing the desert to the west. My father followed, and when he and his men arrived at a port on the Red Sea, they learned that Shêtân—they knew it was he by that time—had been taken on the freighter *Drake,* which later sank off the coast of Spain. He returned knowing full well that his one chance of beating Abd-al-Rahman's chestnut stallion, Sagr, was gone with the death of Shêtân." She paused. "Months later, through my brother in England, my father learned of you and your horse." She turned and looked at Alec. "You know the rest."

"When will the race take place?" Alec asked.

"In three weeks," Tabari replied, "the first day of the new moon."

They stood in silence for a while. Then finally she smiled and said, "I have talked long and it is late." Slowly they made their way back into the house.

Before he went to bed that night, Alec found the others and related to them what Tabari had told him.

Blood Brother

11

That next morning Alec was awakened by a soft knock on the door. One of Abu Ishak's servants walked in and moved silently across the room. As he passed the foot of Alec's bed he turned and smiled, then proceeded to the large windows, where he pulled the long drapes wide open, allowing the early morning sun to flood the room.

He left and a moment later returned with a large tray bearing fruit, which he placed in front of Alec. He retired near the door and stood there in silence.

Luxuriously, Alec stretched in bed and ate.

He thought of Tabari and the story she had told him. He thought of the beauty of Abd-al-Rahman's chestnut stallion, and wondered if Sagr could match the heart and speed of the Black. It would be a race to see! Alec sobered . . . if only the stakes weren't so high. For if Tabari was right, the defeat of the Black would mean much bloodshed. His thoughts turned to Abd-al-Rahman and once more he saw the tall, big-boned Bedouin with the great black beard. Why couldn't he see that Abu Já Kub ben Ishak couldn't have murdered his best friend and his wife and newborn child? Still, there was the knife, and Abd-al-Rahman was young and impetuous. He sought revenge.

Alec's thoughts turned to the gold medallion and the bird that they thought to be the Phoenix. Where did that come in? And was it, by any chance, upon Abd-al-Rahman's orders that the Black had been stolen in order to keep him out of the race, to make certain that Sagr would win? And failing, and knowing that Abu Já Kub ben Ishak was on his way to the United states to bring back Shêtân, did Abd-al-Rahman or one of his men reach the States first and attempt to kill the Black?

They were not pleasant thoughts. He could not think of Abd-al-Rahman as resorting to such treachery. Yet, this was a strange land, and he had much to learn.

As he dressed, his thoughts turned to Tabari and what Henry had told him last night before they had gone to bed. Abu Já Kub ben Ishak had met his wife in the Far East, he had informed Henry and Mr. Volence, and had brought her back with him to the Kharj. She had died three years later after the birth of her second child, Tabari. Abu Ishak had sent both of his children to England to receive their education, but Tabari, unhappy away from her father and her home, had returned after five years. That accounted, anyway, for her well-spoken English.

The others, including Abu Ishak, were waiting for Alec when he arrived downstairs.

"Come," their host said, "we have horses waiting."

Alec fell in beside Henry. "What's it all about?" he asked. "Where are we going?"

"Abu told us this morning about the comin' race, but didn't go into all the details," Henry whispered. "Now we're gonna watch a workout. He thought we'd be interested."

Outside, Bedouins held the horses. Tabari mounted Jôhar, while the filly danced nervously. Then the others mounted and they rode away from the house. Alec pressed his legs around the girth of the dark bay he was riding. It felt good to be back in a saddle. He patted the neck of his horse and let him play with the bit.

Henry rode beside him on a large gray, who shied away from the bay. "Great life, isn't it!" Henry grinned.

They were nearing the grazing band when Alec asked, "Who's riding the Black, Henry?"

"One of Abu's men. Don't know his name." Henry chuckled. "Abu had quite a time, he tells us. After he returned with the Black, he found that none of his riders could manage him. He was in a spot, all right, until one day about a month ago a lone Bedouin arrived in the valley, seeking to become a member of Abu Ishak's clan. Y'know, Alec, Abu tells us that all members of a clan consider themselves of one blood. Kinship is taken care of by suckin' a few drops of another's blood. Mighty interestin', isn't it?" Then without waiting for Alec's reply, he continued, "Anyway, Abu put this new guy on somethin' like a probation period before they let him join up. He turned out to be okay, according to Abu, and also one of the best riders he'd ever seen. Abu put him on the Black one day and sure enough, after a tough fight, which I for one would like to have seen, he gets the Black under control. Abu was plenty relieved 'cause he sure was worried about not having anybody to ride the Black.'' Henry paused. ''I'm lookin' forward to seein' this guy, Alec . . . didn't think it was possible for anybody to ride the Black but you.''

As they neared the grazing band they saw a small group of mounted Bedouins. Suddenly in the center of the group the Black reared, his forelegs pawing the air. The men pulled him down and moved in close.

When Alec and the others arrived, they had the stallion saddled. A white-robed figure with his back to Alec moved quickly from the back of his own horse into the saddle. The Black reared again and the men broke and turned their horses away.

Skillfully, the Black's rider brought him down. The stallion reared again and for a moment Alec thought he would go straight over backwards, crushing the man in the saddle. Moving his body forward, the Bedouin buried his heels in the Black's sides. The stallion bolted forward and with ever increasing strides swept over the ground, his powerful quarters rising and falling.

They watched as the giant horse with pounding hoofs raced around the edge of the valley, the ground slipping away in waves beneath him. The Bedouin, like a small burr, was lost in the flowing black mane. As they neared the group of bystanders once more, Alec saw a whip raised in the Bedouin's hand, and he bit his lip until the blood flowed freely. There was no reason to hit the Black! No need for a whip! The hard leather fell on the giant body. The stallion sprang forward as though unleashed from a spring. As they raced past, Alec saw the whip fall again. Angrily, he turned to Henry. ''He's using a crop," he said and his words were clipped. "The fool!"

Henry looked at Abu Ishak, who was standing beside him. "He'll break your Shêtân if he continues to use a whip," he said.

Abu Ishak's voice, when he answered, was cold and unwavering. "I've never seen him use a crop before . . . and he won't do it again, I assure you." His eyes never left the racing horse.

Horse and rider circled the valley once more, and then the Bedouin gradually slowed down the Black. Fighting for his head, the stallion moved effortlessly toward them, his hot black body glistening in the sun.

Abu Ishak signaled his men as the Black neared them, and they moved out to meet the stallion. The rider dismounted and a blanket was thrown over the horse, who shook his savage head furiously.

Henry mumbled to Alec, "That guy can stick on a horse, but he'll never get the best outa the Black . . . 'cause he'll fight him every inch of the way until his spirit is broken."

Alec did not answer.

Noticing the smoldering look in Alec's eyes, Henry said, "Take it easy, kid. Leave it to Abu, he'll do something about it. He's talking to him now."

They watched as Abu Já Kub ben Ishak called his rider to one side and spoke to him in Arabic. His voice was raised in anger. The sullen dark face of the Bedouin rider was turned up to Abu Ishak, as the tall sheikh towered above him. When Shêtân's owner had finished speaking, the rider nodded and turned away.

They were on their way back across the valley when

Tabari rode up beside Alec. "If you would like," she said, "we can go for a short ride."

Alec nodded. It would do him good to ride for a while.

They broke away from the others, Tabari leading the way. Cantering, they rode to the south end of the valley, and then Tabari turned up a small trail that led through the mountains.

They rode in silence while their horses followed the path which wound its way up to the summit. Suddenly Alec realized that the surroundings were familiar and that they were not far from the narrow chasm through which he and his friends had entered the valley.

Noticing Alec's close scrutiny of the terrain, Tabari smiled and said, "It is safe so long as we do not leave the valley."

They stopped to rest when they reached a clearing. Stretched out below they could see the small figures of the grazing horses and the white buildings to the north.

They had been there only a few minutes when suddenly the horses moved uneasily, their heads raised and ears cocked. Tabari's Jôhar neighed softly. Then they heard the ring of hoofs against stone. Turning, they saw Abd-al-Rahman on the path above, riding his chestnut stallion, Sagr.

Tabari straightened in her saddle, but did not move.

Abd-al-Rahman rode up to them, nodded to Alec, and then spoke to Tabari in Arabic, his voice soft, his brown eyes keen and appraising.

As Alec watched them, he marveled at the courage of this young chieftain who had dared to enter the domain of Abu Já Kub ben Ishak alone. And why? To watch the Black's workout? Perhaps. Or was there some other reason? Tabari had told him she hadn't seen Abd-al-Rahman since the last race . . . five years ago.

The young chieftain laughed and placed a brown hand upon the pommel of Jôhar's saddle. Tabari raised her voice angrily, and her lips trembled.

Alec moved between them. He didn't know what he could do, but he couldn't just stand by. Tabari turned to him.

"He has threatened to ride off with me," she said angrily. "He . . . does not think I have the ability to choose for myself!"

She swept the hand of the young chieftain off her saddle.

Alec was astonished at the wildness and courage of the girl, who was so small that in talking to Abd-al-Rahman she had to throw her head backwards. She was untamed, uncurbed by restraint . . . like Jôhar, the purebred she rode.

He looked at Abd-al-Rahman. His smooth face was boyish and gentle beneath the flowing black beard. It was difficult to believe that this man was responsible for the shedding of blood in the past . . . that he was the man the family and clan of Abu Já Kub ben Ishak feared.

Tabari took up Jôhar's reins, and the sheikh made no move to stop her. His eyes laughed into her angry ones. Her voice rose to a higher and angrier pitch. Then, to Alec's amazement, she suddenly burst into tears, turned Jôhar so quickly that the horse almost fell, and fled.

Alec followed, deep in thought.

Ibn al Khaldun

12

That night Alec found it difficult to sleep. His mind, active and alert, turned to the coming race, Abu Já Kub ben Ishak, Tabari, and Abd-al-Rahman. Then there was the small Bedouin who was to ride the Black in his race against Abd-al-Rahman's chestnut stallion, Sagr. He was a skilled rider, but he would not get the best out of the Black . . . and every bit of speed the great stallion had would be necessary to beat Sagr.

Rolling over on his back, Alec's gaze swept to the windows. Through the heavy drapes he could see the moonlight filtering inside. He closed his eyes and finally slept.

Hours later he suddenly awakened and sat upright in bed. A hand swept across his sleep-laden eyes. Had it been a dream, or had he actually heard the Black scream? Quickly he jumped out of bed and walked to the window. Pulling the drapes to one side, he looked up the valley. All was quiet, and a dull gray in the east marked the coming of dawn. He went back, but sleep would not come.

A shrill whistle pierced the night air. The Black!

Alec ran to the window. To the others, if they had heard, it was only the scream of a wild stallion. But to Alec, the high-pitched whistle meant danger . . . danger to the Black. He had heard it before.

In the gray light he could see the horses bunched together up the valley. They moved slowly at first, then faster into a gallop. Breaking away from them was the giant form of the Black. As Alec's eyes became accustomed to the light, he made out a figure on the back of the stallion. The Black ran in spurts, stopping, whirling, vainly attempting to unseat his rider.

Pulling on his clothes quickly, Alec hurried downstairs. He stopped when he reached Abu Ishak's bedroom and pounded on the door. It was opened a moment later by the tall sheikh.

"The Black . . . Shêtân . . . I saw someone riding him!"

Sleep vanished from Abu Ishak's black eyes as he looked into Alec's taut face. "Go to the stables. . . . Awaken my men there. . . . Bring horses. I'll meet you in front."

The valley was quiet when Alec left the house and ran toward the stables. As far as he could see, there was no sign of the Black."

When he returned with the horses and sleepy Bedouins, Abu Ishak was waiting for them. He mounted and they rode swiftly toward the grazing band.

The horses moved nervously as the riders approached them, then broke into a gallop. The Bedouins headed them off and they thundered past Alec and Abu Ishak.

Abu's eyes shifted to Alec. The Black was not among them.

"In which direction, Alec?" Abu Ishak asked, and his voice was as cold as the steel dagger he bore on his belt.

"He was more to the west when I saw him . . ."

Abu Já Kub ben Ishak shouted to his men, and then they rode. When they had gone a short distance, Abu stopped his horse and dismounted. Closely he scrutinized the ground, then mounted again. Alec and the others followed as the sheikh led them down the valley. They turned up the path which Alec recognized as the one he and Tabari had taken the day before . . . the one that led to the narrow chasm, which in turn led to the outer world.

They climbed rapidly, pushing their horses to keep up with Abu Ishak. Finally they reached the clearing and came to a halt. Abu sat straight in his saddle; his keen eyes moved from the chasm above across the surrounding terrain.

Suddenly he kicked his horse forward and headed up the trail. He made an abrupt turn as they neared the chasm, came to a stop, and dismounted. When Alec arrived, he saw him bending over the body of a white-robed figure. As Abu stepped to one side, Alec saw the large blood stain between the shoulder blades.

Abu Já Kub ben Ishak looked up at him, and spoke in a grim, clipped voice. "The sentry whose nightly post this was . . . is dead." His voice rose. "Before Allah, this time it is the end!'' He leaped into his saddle without using the stirrup, and pulled his gray into a rear. Up and down it plunged, as Abu swore and roared angrily at his men, who turned and rode swiftly down the trail. Abu Ishak turned to Alec. ''Come,'' he said curtly, ''we go back.''

They rode in silence, and when they reached Abu Ishak's home the sun had risen above the mountains to the east. Abu dismounted and without a word to Alec entered the house.

Alec remained in his saddle. The Black was gone . . . stolen again. What would Abu Já Kub ben Ishak do this time? The sentry was dead. Blood had been shed . . . and blood called for blood. The law of the desert. Abd-al-Rahman in the valley the day before . . . had he returned?

A Bedouin ran past him and entered the house. There was a tenseness in the air, and suddenly a drum boomed, its rhythmic beats echoing throughout the valley. Horses were being saddled in the stables, and from the homes white-robed figures appeared carrying saddles and guns. The pounding of hoofs attracted Alec's attention to the valley. The horses were being driven in by swift-riding Bedouins.

The men of Abu Já Kub ben Ishak were preparing for battle!

Alec sat still in his saddle, listening to the incessant beating of the drum, which seemed to say over and over . . . ''Blood for Blood. . . . Blood for Blood.''

Swiftly the men of Abu Já Kub ben Ishak gathered a short distance from the house. Their women brought ammunition and food to them. Guns were fired to clear them. Horses neighed and tramped restlessly. They were assembled and ready to follow their sheikh.

Abu Já Kub ben Ishak appeared on the porch; behind him were Tabari and the others. He raised his hand for silence, then spoke to them. Finishing, he turned to Tabari and together they walked toward his gray.

Alec was suddenly aware of Raj beside him. "Does this mean war with Abd-al-Rahman?" Alec asked grimly.

To Alec's surprise his friend shook his head. "No, not necessarily, although Abu Já Kub ben Ishak has told his men that the trail may lead to Abd-al-Rahman, and they go prepared. It is one of their own clan that they seek, their blood brother who was to ride the Black in the race, for it is he who is missing, and he who has stolen Shêtân and killed his brother."

"So it was he," Alec muttered. The man had become affiliated with the clan of Abu Já Kub ben Ishak for this sole purpose, Alec was certain. But why? Certainly he did not think he could cross the desert and sell the Black before Abu Ishak and his men found him. The most obvious answer was that he was in the employ of Abd-al-Rahman, who had good reason to do away with the Black. Alec clasped the gold chain and medallion which were deep in the pocket of his white gown. Perhaps it was Abd-al-Rahman or one of his men who had attempted to kill the Black back home. Perhaps the boyish face and kind eyes of Abd-al-Rahman belied the savage and ruthless heart that beat within his giant frame. Perhaps it was his nature to be brutal when there was a chance that he and his horse might be beaten.

Alec turned in his saddle and saw that Abu Ishak and

his men were ready to leave. His gaze shifted to Henry and Mr. Volence standing on the porch, then back to Abu.

"You go with them?" Raj asked in a soft, tense voice.

Alec, deep in thought, did not hear Raj's question.

Abu Já Kub ben Ishak raised his hand and drove his spurs into his gray stallion. His men followed behind him, and riding in no particular formation, they swept down the valley.

Alec drew the reins hard against the neck of his horse and set out after them without a backward glance. Yes, he knew what he was doing, he told himself . . . knew also what he might be getting into. But his horse had been stolen; and he had to join the others in their search for him. He couldn't sit back and wait . . . again. He could help, in some way. The backs of the white-robed figures in front rose and fell with the hindquarters of their horses. Because of his clothing, they wouldn't know he was not one of them until it was too late to send him back.

He followed as the Bedouins, forming a single line, rode up the path that led to the chasm in the mountains above. He turned in his saddle at the sound of a running horse to his rear. Another Bedouin! As he drew closer, Alec saw that it was Raj. The young Bedouin raised his hand, and fell in behind Alec. "I go with you," he said.

They had to push their horses to catch up with the riders ahead. Soon they reached the clearing where they had found the dead sentry. Then they went on to the chasm and filed through it until they had reached the outer ravine. The men rode more slowly now, their guns unslung and placed across their thighs.

At times they would stop while Abu Já Kub ben Ishak and his men inspected the ground. Then, after a few minutes, they would advance again, very often changing the direction of their march. The men rode easily, and still in no particular formation.

That night they camped thirty miles away from the valley of Abu Já Kub ben Ishak.

Alec and Raj unsaddled their horses a short distance away from the others, and stretched out on the ground. "Perhaps it is best that we make ourselves known," Raj suggested softly. "We cannot go much farther without food."

Alec nodded, and his gaze turned toward Abu Ishak. The sheikh was moving among his men. Each handed him his gun, and Abu Ishak would check the sights and then give it back to the owner. As he neared them, Alec said, "Here he comes, Raj, whether we like it or not."

The stern expression on Abu Ishak's face did not change when he saw and recognized them. He showed no surprise, and his voice was calm. "Why did you come?" he asked.

"To help you find Shêtân," Alec replied, his eyes unwavering as they met those of the sheikh.

"Âfferin! So the little cock crows. He grows spurs. He is going to help Abu Já Kub ben Ishak and his men. Listen, my young friend, this is no peaceful country we ride through so cautiously. It is a land forbidden to men of all races, all colors." A thin smile flickered on his lips and his eyes lost much of their sternness as he added, "But yes, I like your crowing. It is a good sign. I would send you back here and now, but then I would have to send one of my men with you, and Allah knows that I cannot do that for I may need every man." He paused. "It is best that you come with us. You will learn much of war and the ways of men beyond the desert."

For two more days they moved easily, and on the third the formation changed. The Bedouins formed a single line and rode from ten to fifteen yards behind one another. As Raj dropped behind Alec, he said, "I was told last night that we have lost the spoor of Shêtân. We near the kingdom of Abd-al-Rahman, and the men are certain that it is there Abu Já Kub ben Ishak will go in search of his horse. If there is opposition on the part of Abd-al-Rahman, it may mean war, Alec." Raj's face was grave as he finished.

They rode on. The Bedouins had one hand placed upon their long guns, for Abu Ishak had passed the word back to be on the alert. As they went forward at a faster pace, a thousand thoughts occupied Alec's mind. He was going to war. The thought frightened him, but there was no turning back. That he would have to take an actual part in the battle had not entered his mind when he had set out with the Bedouins. He and Raj were unarmed, and no match for the hardened warriors of Abd-al-Rahman.

Finally they reached a plain and rode straight across it, still in the same formation. The Bedouins spurred their horses into a gallop and the ground shook from the thundering hoofs. It was early afternoon when Alec saw a large mass of rock ahead. Abu Já Kub ben Ishak raised his hand and his men slowed their horses. They moved cautiously forward, and Alec realized that before them was the stronghold of Abd-al-Rahman!

It was clearly visible now. The reddish rock rose in sheer cliffs above the plain, making the stronghold, it seemed to Alec, practically impregnable. Certainly the men of Abd-al-Rahman, firing from the top of the cliffs, could withstand an army many times the size of theirs.

Abu Já Kub ben Ishak brought his men to a halt about a quarter of a mile away from the rocks. He raised his rifle and fired three times. Then he sat back in his saddle and waited with the others, their keen eyes upon the stronghold ahead.

Not long after, a horseman appeared, followed by three others. They rode cautiously toward Abu Ishak and his men.

As they approached, Alec made out the flowing black beard of Abd-al-Rahman. He rode straight in his saddle, his gun unslung and held in one hand. Sagr's pale golden mane and tail whipped in the breeze that blew across the plain. Abd-al-Rahman stopped when he was a short distance from them, and Abu Já Kub ben Ishak rode forth to meet him.

Alec saw the two sheikhs raise their hands in salute, then Abu Já Kub ben Ishak spoke. Raj, standing near Alec, whispered, "He is explaining why we have come. His words are strong."

Alec's gaze shifted to the mounted Bedouin to the right and just behind Abd-al-Rahman. There had been something familiar about him. He moved closer to get a better view and Raj followed.

The Bedouin sat back in his saddle. He carried no gun and, unlike the others, held the reins in his right hand. Alec looked for the man's left arm, and could find none!

Quickly his eyes swept to the Bedouin's face. It was difficult to make out his features under the low head shawl. Alec moved still closer.

He stopped. He could not be mistaken. The Bedouin behind Abd-al-Rahman was Ibn al Khaldun! Sweat was pouring down the fatty crevices of his face as he stared into the sun. His lips were pulled back, disclosing the toothless gums, as he listened to the words of Abu Já Kub ben Ishak.

Alec moved cautiously back to the others. He hoped Ibn al Khaldun had not recognized him. Ibn al Khaldun here, one of the clan of Abd-al-Rahman! Ibn al Khaldun on the plane, leaving the States not long after the attack on the Black! The medallion, which he wore around his neck, the same as the one found in the barn after the attack on the Black! Everything tied together.

Raj touched him on the shoulder. "They have finished," he said.

Sagr reared as Abd-al-Rahman's long limbs squeezed about his girth. The young Bedouin chief touched his neck with the rein. Sagr whirled, and without a backward glance Abd-al-Rahman rode toward his stronghold, followed by his men.

Abu Já Kub ben Ishak watched them for a minute, then turned back to his men, his face stern and cold.

"Abd-al-Rahman," Raj explained to Alec, "claims to know nothing of the disappearance of Shêtân. Abu Já Kub ben Ishak does not believe him and he told him so in words that were as sharp as the point of his dagger. If Shêtân is not returned by the time the sun rises above the mountains tomorrow morning he will attack the stronghold of Abd-al-Rahman." Raj's eyes turned to the mass of rocks piled high on top of one another. "Much blood will be shed, Alec, if the sun rises without Shêtân's being returned."

Abu Já Kub ben Ishak spoke to his men, and when he had finished they dismounted and made camp. The tall sheikh then walked up to Alec and Raj. "It is best that you go now," he said. "You will be taken to the mountains to the south end of the plains, and there you will wait until we have finished." Without further word he turned to leave.

Alec stopped him and proceeded to tell him about Ibn al Khaldun: how they had traveled with him in the plane from the States, and of the gold medallion which he wore around his neck.

"It is as I thought," Abu Já Kub ben Ishak said. "The arms of Abd-al-Rahman are long."

He left then, and a few minutes later a Bedouin rode up and motioned Alec and Raj to mount. As they rode past the men, Alec could not help being surprised at their calmness. The coming battle seemed no great adventure to them. The horses, unsaddled, had been watered and were grazing. The Bedouins seemed content with the world; they sat on the ground, smoking, talking. Some even slept, their head shawls pulled down over their faces to shade them from the scorching sun. Only Abu Já Kub ben Ishak moved among them, once more checking their guns, their ammunition, and his head did not turn toward Alec and Raj as they passed.

Alec stared at the rocks behind him. How many men did Abd-al-Rahman have in his stronghold? Would they come forth to battle on the plain or would Abu Ishak's men have to scale the cliffs? Many of the men who now

were stretched contentedly on the ground would probably be dead before the sun set the following day. Didn't
that matter to them? Were they so hardened that they
never even gave it a thought? His gaze shifted back to
the horses as they moved slowly in their grazing, their
long, slender necks bent to the ground. Centuries had
been spent in their careful breeding, yet many of them,
too, would be dead the following day. Abu Ishak had
bred them for war or racing . . . and war had come
first.

Renegades

13

Riding swiftly behind the Bedouin, who seemed anxious to return to the others, they reached the mountains to the south in an hour. There the guide left them.

Alone, Raj and Alec looked at each other, their faces grave.

"Guess all we can do now is wait," Alec said.

"*Ê* . . . yes," Raj replied, then added, "If we were to ascend the mountain a short way, we should be able to see them."

Alec nodded, and moved his horse. A short while later they arrived at a small overhanging plateau, where they stopped and dismounted. In the distance they could make out Abu Ishak's men, and still farther ahead the stronghold of Abd-al-Rahman. They waited in silence, both thinking of the battle that would be held the following morning.

The sun was still high in the heavens when Alec felt Raj's hand on his arm. He rose to his feet and shielded his eyes from the rays of the sun. "Look to the west of the rocks, Alec, to the side away from the men of Abu Já Kub ben Ishak. Is that not a figure on horseback emerging from the stronghold of Abd-al-Rahman?"

Alec stood beside his friend and looked in the direction in which he was pointing. It was several minutes before he could see anything in the glare of the sun, then his eyes made out the moving figure. "Yes, Raj," he said, "I see him now."

They watched as the horseman made his way to the western edge of the plain, then turned to the south. "He's coming this way," Alec muttered.

"He goes around the men of Abu Já Kub ben Ishak," Raj said. "They cannot see him for he is farther away than their eyes can observe."

Alec nodded.

An hour passed, and without changing direction, keeping close to the western mountain range, the horseman came down the plain.

"He does not ride like Abd-al-Rahman. It is not he," Raj said.

"No. Nor is it Sagr, for this horse is black," mused Alec.

The horseman was less than a quarter of a mile away. He was pushing his horse hard. Suddenly he left the cover of the mountains and headed straight in their direction.

"It is as though he makes for the trail below," Raj said. "It is best that we hide."

Alec said nothing. His eyes watched the hard-riding

figure. He was getting close now. The reins! They were held in the rider's right hand! A left hand? Alec could see none. His fists clenched until white showed beneath his deeply tanned skin. "Raj!" he shouted. "It's Ibn al Khaldun!"

"He turns toward the path," Raj said. "Come, we must hide or he will see us."

Quickly they led their horses away from the trail and into the dense brush. There they waited. "He will not be able to see us here," Raj said.

Tossing their leads, the horses moved uneasily; ears pricked quickly forward. "We must keep them quiet," Alec warned, rubbing the soft muzzle of his horse.

The ringing sound of hoofs against stone came closer. Peering out of the brush, Alec and Raj saw the bobbing head of the horse, his eyes prominent in his head and white lather standing out against his black neck. Ibn al Khaldun sat heavily on his back, his broad shoulders hunched forward.

He reached the level plateau, and without resting, drove his horse onto the trail above.

Alec and Raj waited in silence until the sound of hoofs could be heard no more. "He's up to something," Alec said. "Wonder what it is?"

Raj shrugged his shoulders. "It is not good, Alec, for he rides hard."

Alec fumbled with the reins, then said, "Raj, let's follow him. We have time, and I have a feeling . . ."

"$\hat{E}$ . . . yes, but we must be careful, Alec. He is a treacherous man from all you have told me of him."

Without another word they mounted and started up the trail, Raj leading the way. They rode cautiously without pushing their horses. When they reached the summit, Raj stopped and dismounted. Closely he inspected the terrain, then mounted again. He beckoned Alec to follow and turned off the trail. They rode down a small ravine for over an hour, then Raj turned up a well worn path that led up the side of a steep cliff. They slowed their horses to a walk. Turning in his saddle, Raj said, "I do not think he is far ahead now, make note of the worn trail. Many horses have traveled on it."

A short while later the trail narrowed as it wound its way among overhanging rocks. Then as they turned a bend the trail widened and led into a long canyon. Raj stopped and dismounted. "It is best that I go ahead by foot," he said. "Wait."

A short time later he returned. The muscles in his face were taut as he said, "Ahead is a village and many men, Alec. I did not see Ibn al Khaldun, but that he is there, I am certain. Let us hide our horses and go by foot through the rocks. We can get very close and still remain unobserved."

Under the protection of the large rocks they made their way slowly up the canyon. Alec, following the slouched figure of his friend, wondered about the men hidden away in this isolated canyon. Where did they fit into the picture? Were they Abd-al-Rahman's men? Had Ibn al Khaldun come here to tell them of the impending battle? If so, Alec knew that it would be likely that they would attack from the rear the following day.

They were near the floor of the canyon, and Alec, afraid that they would be discovered, whispered, "Let's go higher, Raj, we're too close."

The Bedouin youth shook his head. "We will not be

observed, Alec. The village is concealed in a hollow and under the large cliff ahead. We can be almost in it without being seen."

A few minutes later they clambered up the cleft of a large rock. "You can see it now, Alec, but be careful as we are only a few feet away from them."

Cautiously, Alec peered through the fissure in the rock. The village consisted of only one long, straggly street of dirty huts. Men, unclean and scarred, stood in small groups; some shouted in high-pitched quarrel-some voices, their hands heavy on the butts of their guns; still others, unmindful of it all, ate hungrily, using daggers for knives. A large corral was behind the hut nearest Alec and Raj, and the horses in it were lean and unkempt with long manes and tails.

There was an air of evil throughout the valley. Alec knew that these were men of whom he had heard from Mr. Coggins, from Raj. They were deserters, runaways . . . men who had been cast out from their tribes, and who had been fortunate to escape with their heads. What were they doing here? Certainly even Abd-al-Rahman would not sink so low as to harbor such a clan. Or would he?

A figure walked out of the hut in front of the corral. "Raj! There's Ibn al Khaldun!" Alec whispered.

With mincing steps, which carried his heavy body amazingly fast over the ground, he came toward them. The men standing about looked at him sullenly and lowered their voices. Ibn al Khaldun did not appear to notice, nor did he deviate from his direction which took him past them. He stopped a short distance away from the rock behind which Alec and Raj were hiding. As though undecided as to his next move he stood there. Then, removing a silk handkerchief from the pocket of his robe, he rubbed it across his perspiring face.

Alec moved uneasily in his crouched position. Had he seen them?

Ibn al Khaldun suddenly turned toward his men and in a loud, harsh voice called one of them. There was a movement in a small group and a Bedouin of slight frame rose from his seat on the ground, scraped his dish clean of food with his dagger, and brought it to his mouth. Swallowing, he threw the dish down, wiped the dagger on his grimy robe, and walked forward.

Alec grasped Raj by the shoulder. For the Bedouin walking toward Ibn al Khaldun was the man who had stolen the Black and killed the sentry . . . the man for whom Abu Já Kub ben Ishak and his warriors were searching! Alec's heart pounded madly. If he was here, then the Black was here! His gaze shifted quickly to the corral, but there was no sign of the stallion. Ibn al Khaldun! Perhaps he had already done away with the Black! Still, he'd only just arrived. . . . He hadn't had much time.

The sound of Ibn al Khaldun's voice raised high in anger attracted Alec's attention to the swarthy Bedouin. The deserter from the tribe of Abu Ishak was cringing in front of him.

Ibn al Khaldun suddenly reached down and with his one hand grabbed the slim Bedouin by the neck. He pulled him off his feet, and in a single movement tore a chain from his neck, and threw him backwards to the ground.

Then he stood over him, the chain dangling from his fat hand.

Alec's throat tightened, for hanging on the gold chain was a medallion . . . *the* medallion!

As Ibn al Khaldun spoke to the Bedouin at his feet, the others slunk forward, only evil and viciousness written on their countenances.

"Raj," Alec whispered, "tell me what he says."

His friend nodded and spoke softly, his eyes upon the moving lips of Ibn al Khaldun. "He says the Bedouin rider has not obeyed his orders, and for that he must die. He was to have stayed in the valley of Abu Já Kub ben Ishak until the race was run. He was to have held Shêtân back so the chestnut stallion, Sagr, could easily have won."

The slim Bedouin, his pupils dilated with fear, grabbed Ibn al Khaldun's leg and babbled hysterically.

Raj began again. "He claims that it was impossible for him to hold back Shêtân . . . that the best Bedouin rider would be overmounted on Shêtân . . . that not even with a heavy bit had it been possible for him to control the stallion. And Abu Já Kub ben Ishak had learned that he had used the heavy bit against his instructions . . . had seen him try to break the spirit of Shêtân with a crop. He had become suspicious. The only way left had been to steal Shêtân. And why was it not better this way? The men of Abu Já Kub ben Ishak would not find Shêtân in the corral up the canyon, which was strong and high enough to hold him. And when the sun rose on the new day, the tribes of Abd-al-Rahman and Abu Já Kub ben Ishak would battle. Much blood would be shed, many would die. And when the battle waned and even the victors were exhausted from loss of blood, they could descend upon them in all their fury and kill them all. Was not that what he wanted?"

Raj stopped. He and Alec watched Ibn al Khaldun as he struck the man at his feet, knocking him unconscious. Then Khaldun turned to the others and his small pig-eyes swept over them. Finally he spoke, his voice harsh and threatening.

Alec, his eyes still on Ibn al Khaldun, listened as Raj interpreted for him. "He says that by Allah, he is still their leader, that he will do their thinking for them. Let no others disobey his orders, or they will suffer the same as the one at his feet. Had they forgotten that they were murderers, who by themselves could not have lived a day outside the confines of this canyon? Were they so blind that they could not still see the furrowed scars on their bodies? Had they forgotten the floggings they had received in payment for their crimes? Did they not remember, one and all, coming to him in fear, pleading for protection from those whom they had wronged?"

Raj stopped as Ibn al Khaldun raised the gold medallion over his head for all to see. Then he spoke again, and Raj continued, "He says that for years they have looked forward to the day when, like the Phoenix, they too would rise again with strong powerful wings. But to rule the mountains and the desert, they would first have to destroy the kingdoms of Abd-al-Rahman and Abu Já Kub ben Ishak; this he had told the first of them twenty years ago. They were few then and not strong, but he, Ibn al Khaldun, had planned well. Had they not murdered the mother, the father, the warriors of Abd-al-Rahman in the desert? And had he not thought to leave Abu Ishak's dagger behind, knowing well that the young son of Abd-al-Rahman, who bore his name, would seek vengeance upon Abu Já Kub ben Ishak, the man his father thought to be his best friend?''

Raj turned to Alec; their eyes were filled with hate. For here was a man capable of anything . . . a man who had carefully plotted the destruction of the tribes of Abd-al-Rahman and Abu Ishak. And if he succeeded there would be no stopping him. He and his bank of outlaws would ravage the mountains and desert, pillaging and killing.

Ibn al Khaldun spoke again, and Raj continued, "He says that if the Bedouin lying at his feet had followed orders, the chestnut stallion of Abd-al-Rahman would have won the race and the best of Abu Já Kub ben Ishak's horses. It would then have been the time to strike, for he had carefully planned the death of Abd-al-Rahman. And upon his death he, Ibn al Khaldun, first cousin of Abd-al-Rahman, would become the sheikh. Then it would have been easy to bring them into the tribe, and, better mounted, they could have destroyed the clan of Abu Já Kub ben Ishak! And gone on and on . . . until the Kharj district was theirs.

''But now his plans had to be changed for, on the plain beyond, the men of Abd-al-Rahman and Abu Já Kub ben Ishak would battle tomorrow. Yes, they would attack as the battle waned, but by Allah it would be difficult for they were undermounted. Still, they would attack with all the fury of their scarred bodies for it was not an opportunity to miss! And they would first seek Abd-al-

Rahman and Abu Já Kub ben Ishak, if they were still alive, and run their spears through them. Yes, and there was another who they must make sure died before the battle ended . . . a Bedouin youth, his face unlined, who rides a roan with a white forehead."

Raj's voice faltered. Alec turned to him for he knew that Raj rode such a horse. But his friend's eyes were fastened on Ibn al Khaldun and he continued interpreting. "It will not be difficult for you to recognize him. He is taller than the others and his cheekbones are high. When you get close in battle you will see that he looks like Abd-al-Rahman . . . and rightly so . . . for he is his *brother*."

The muscles in Raj's face bulged, his mouth opened. Alec placed a hand on his friend's shoulder. "Easy, Raj," he said, "we can do nothing now."

Raj turned and his voice at first was bewildered as he said slowly, "Then I . . . I was the newborn babe Ibn al Khaldun could not find . . . to murder." Then it became choked with bitterness and hate as he added vehemently, "This man, Alec . . . *he* is responsible for the death of my mother and father . . ."

"I know, Raj, I know . . . and you will have your revenge. We have heard enough. We must get back to warn the others." Alec paused, his eyes seeking his friends. "Aren't you scared, Raj?"

"No, for neither Ibn al Khaldun nor his men shall kill me. It is they who will learn the meaning of fear; it is they who will quake and fall to their knees before the fury of my people. We go to tell my brother what we have heard . . . and then we return."

Their gaze turned once again to Ibn al Khaldun, who

was walking in the direction of his hut, followed by two scarred Bedouins carrying the limp figure of the man who was to pay with his life for disobeying orders.

The others returned to their groups, and soon high-pitched voices resumed the quarrels Ibn al Khaldun had interrupted.

They had crawled from the rock, and Raj was already moving on his way back down the canyon, when Alec placed a hand on his shoulder. "Raj," he said, "you go . . . one of us ought to stay here. Besides, you'll travel faster alone."

Raj met his friend's gaze. "You mean, you are going up the canyon to find the corral that holds Shêtân?"

"Maybe. It would be like Ibn al Khaldun to do away with the Black before the attack."

"No, I do not think so," Raj whispered. "For he is undermounted, as he himself said. He needs good horses."

"But he's going to kill the only man who can ride him," Alec reminded him.

Raj shrugged his shoulders. "Stay if you wish, Alec," he said. "I will return with many men before the moon rises above the mountains. The men here will be sleeping. It should not be difficult." Raj turned and moved quickly away.

Captured!

14

After Raj left, Alec slowly made his way through the
rocks toward the upper canyon. Somewhere ahead was
the Black! His brain whirled from the rapidity with
which everything had fallen into place. Now he knew
the reason for the attack on the Black . . . knew why
Ibn al Khaldun had wanted him done away with. For Ibn
al Khaldun, learning that Abu Já Kub ben Ishak was on
his way to the United States to claim his horse, had
arrived there first and attempted to kill the Black. Yet
the great stallion was but a small pawn in the complex,
deadly game Ibn al Khaldun was playing! . . . Raj had to
get through, . . . Alec was certain he would. Raj . . .
the brother of Abd-al-Rahman. It was a little difficult to
believe at first . . . yet as Alec thought about it, and
recalled the similarity in the features of the two, so
different from the other Bedouins, he wondered that he
had not guessed the truth before.

It was almost dark when Alec decided he had gone far enough and should see what was in the canyon below. Cautiously, he approached the rim. About a mile down the canyon he could see the village and the men still grouped around the huts. At first he could see nothing below him in the ever deepening shadows, then he made out a narrow gorge that ran up the side of the mountain, only to come to an abrupt end as it met a sheer wall of stone. As Alec's eyes became more accustomed to the dwindling light he made out a high wooden gate at the entrance of the gorge. This could be the corral for which he was searching!

Finding a narrow ledge that led down the side of the canyon, he set out. He moved slowly, his eyes on the precarious trail ahead. Stopping to rest halfway down, he looked in the direction of the village. It could not be seen. Shrugging his shoulders with relief, he started down again.

Reaching the floor of the canyon, he proceeded more cautiously than before, for the rocks no longer hid him from prying eyes, and he did not know if Ibn al Khaldun had placed a guard there.

He was nearing the gate when he heard the sound of pounding hoofs. Alec flattened himself against the rocks. As he stood there he saw the Black appear behind the gate, his head high and ears cocked. He turned in Alec's direction and tossed his head.

Alec's first impulse was to run to his horse, but he restrained himself and remained still. His eyes moved around the canyon for the sign of a sentry. The stallion neighed and shook his head more furiously. Minutes passed. The Black reared, bringing his forelegs down upon the gate, which reached high above his head.

Alec moved forward quickly for he realized the Black might easily break a leg. At sight of him, the stallion shrilled loudly, and brought his forelegs down to the ground. Running to him, Alec shoved his arms through the long, wooden bars. Bending his head, the stallion nuzzled Alec, who rubbed the soft skin.

Alec looked anxiously down the canyon. The Black's scream could easily have attracted the attention of the men in the village. He had to work fast! Untying the rope which held the gate closed, he swung it open. The stallion crab-stepped through and pushed him with his head. Alec swung him around alongside the gate, climbed a few bars, and then leaped on the back of the stallion, his fingers grasping the heavy mane.

For a monent, Alec forgot the dangers before him . . . forgot everything except the thrill of once again being astride the Black, whose sensitive body quivered at the touch of his knees. It was as though the stallion had missed him as well, for he stood quite still, his head up and ears cocked.

Fortunately night had fallen fast and Alec knew that it would be difficult for anyone to see them. He gave the Black his head, but kept him to a walk. He rode away from the village, hoping to find another exit from the narrow canyon. If he found none, he decided he would wait in the protective darkness of the night until the moon rose above the mountains . . . until Raj returned with the warriors of Abu Já Kub ben Ishak and Abd-al-Rahman.

After Raj left Alec, he moved swiftly and with little caution down the canyon. When he reached the horses, he mounted his, and savagely threw the roan back onto its haunches. His anxious, boyish expression was gone and his eyes smoldered with anger. Then he rode hard, a heavy hand on his mount.

A sense of new strength and power coursed through his veins. No longer was he Raj, the houseboy of Mr. Coggins of Haribwan, a nameless youth to be pitied. *La* . . . no! He was the brother of Abd-al-Rahman, powerful sheikh of the Kharj! And together they would seek vengeance upon Ibn al Khaldun for the murder of their father and mother.

Night had fallen by the time Raj reached the small plateau from which he and Alec had first seen Ibn al Khaldun. His horse stumbled and grabbed at the bit. Recovering, Raj drove him down the trail to the plain below.

No fires burned in the camp of Abu Já Kub ben Ishak, but Raj knew the men were there . . . somewhere in the darkness . . . waiting vigilantly for the coming dawn. The roan responded as Raj gave him his head, and they swept down the plain.

A short time later he slowed his horse to a walk, for not far ahead was his brother's stronghold and Abu Ishak's men must be near even though he could not see them.

The roan pranced nervously, his body hot under Raj's long limbs. Suddenly, there was the sharp click of a rifle bolt in the darkness to the left. A voice ordered him to halt.

Raj explained that it was important that he be taken to Abu Já Kub ben Ishak at once.

An unmounted Bedouin appeared, leading his horse. He peered at Raj closely. Recognizing him, he nodded, and motioned him to follow. They moved silently across the plain a short way. Then Raj made out the figures of a small group of men. He and the Bedouin sentry passed them and soon came to another group, which they also passed. Raj realized then that Abu Ishak, to avoid any chance of a surprise attack on the part of Abd-al-Rahman, had scattered his men.

Finally they stopped and the sentry told Raj to wait. A few minutes later he returned and with him was the tall, slim figure of Abu Já Kub ben Ishak, his white beard sharply outlined in the darkness.

Raj, his voice strained with emotion, informed him in his native tongue of all that he and Alec had learned.

Abu Já Kub ben Ishak listened without interruption. When Raj had finished his long story, Abu Ishak remained silent. Then in a cold voice he told Raj to follow and led the way back to his men. There he gave orders to his men to light fires and assemble. Taking his long rifle, he raised it in the air and fired a volley of three shots. Then he lighted a flare and, holding it, mounted his gray stallion. He motioned Raj to follow, and together they rode toward the stronghold of Abd-al-Rahman.

They stopped halfway and waited, their figures silhouetted against the darkness by the burning flare held in the raised hand of Abu Já Kub ben Ishak.

The minutes passed . . . then out of the night came the hoofs of running horses. Suddenly they stopped and were no more. Raj realized that the horsemen, wary of a trap, had brought their mounts to a halt. Then trotting horses moved to the left, others to the right. Coming directly toward them were the prancing but restrained hoofbeats of a walking horse.

Raj stared into the darkness as the hoofbeats ahead became more pronounced. Then the small head and golden mane of Sagr appeared in the light cast from the flaming torch. On his back sat Abd-al-Rahman, his rifle unslung and ready in his hand. "This man," thought Raj, "is of my own flesh and blood . . . my brother."

Abd-al-Rahman stopped a few yards away from them and his inquisitive eyes met those of the older sheikh. Abu Já Kub ben Ishak was the first to speak, and he told Abd-al-Rahman what he had learned from Raj. As Abd-al-Rahman listened his eyes narrowed and his mouth bacame hard and set, forming a thin line. His gaze shifted to Raj when Abu Ishak told him that the youth with him was his brother, but his face disclosed no emotion.

When the story was finished, Abd-al-Rahman jerked his chestnut stallion into a rear. Up and down it plunged, as angry as its rider. Abd-al-Rahman swore as Sagr bucketed underneath him. He would first make certain Abu Ishak was telling him the truth, he shouted. He would return to his home and if Ibn al Khaldun was not to be found, he and his warriors would go with them to the canyon of which be had been told! Abd-al-Rahman flung Sagr around and disappeared into the darkness.

Raj returned with Abu Já Kub ben Ishak to his men, who were now busily checking their arms and saddling their horses. They did not have long to wait before many lighted torches appeared, one following another, from the stronghold of Abd-al-Rahman.

"They come forth," Abu Já Kub ben Ishak said to Raj. Then, turning to his men, he ordered them to mount.

As the thunder of pounding hoofs shook the ground beneath and the seemingly endless line of flares pierced the darkness, Raj took the rifle Abu Já Kub ben Ishak handed him. Tonight the clans of Abd-al-Rahman and Abu Já Kub ben Ishak would ride together again . . . this time to avenge the death of his own father and mother. And he would ride beside his brother in battle! It was as his father would have wanted it. The moon was still behind the mountains and by the time it rose they would be at the canyon, as he had told Alec, his friend.

The canyon narrowed as Alec rode slowly in the night, the walls of stone gradually closing in upon him and his horse. If there was another way out, it was going to be difficult to find. Suddenly the Black shied and Alec felt the giant body tremble. He looked into the darkness but could see nothing. The stallion shied again, his nostrils quivering.

Alec placed a hand upon the high crest of the Black's neck, attempting to calm him. Something was up, he thought, although in the blackness of the canyon he could not see any sign of movement. He brought the stallion to a halt, but the big horse would not remain still. His hoofs played nervously on the ground.

Sensing danger ahead, Alec turned the Black and went back the way he had come. The stallion attempted to break out of the running walk at which Alec held him. Having no reins or bridle, it was difficult for Alec to hold his horse back. He talked to him, pushing his head close to the stallion's neck.

The Black broke into a fast trot, his head up and ears pricked. Realizing that they were again nearing the corral, Alec attempted to bring the stallion to a stop, but to no avail. He moved forward on the horse's back and placed a hand between the pricked ears. He had to stop him or soon it would be too late.

Suddenly the Black came to an abrupt halt and half-reared. Alec grasped the long mane and held on. The stallion snorted and turned up the canyon. He ran a short way, then stopped again and stood still. His head turned up the canyon, then down. Once again he moved, this time in the direction of the east wall; he stopped when he could go no farther. He stood there against the high cliff, his giant body trembling.

Alec was certain there was danger both up and down the canyon, even though he had not seen or heard anything. He stroked the neck of his horse. If they were still perhaps in the darkness they would not be discovered.

The stallion moved uneasily and occasionally there would be a sharp ring as his hoofs kicked a stone. Minutes passed, then the Black suddenly began pawing the ground with his foreleg. Alec thought he heard the sound of hoofs in the darkness. The stallion broke, ran a few yards to the north, then whirled, swept back, and again stood still.

Then the sound of hoofs closing in on them was unmistakable. They came from directly ahead, from the north, and from the south. Alec peered in the darkness, certain that the horses were less than fifty yards away.

Alec hesitated until he saw the mounted figures. There were three of them coming toward him. The Black snorted and reared. When he came down, Alec gave him his head. Bolting, the stallion headed for the men. They would have to break through! Where they would turn after that Alec did not know.

The horsemen moved in on them from three sides. Alec swung the Black around to the south. In a few seconds the stallion, now gathering himself, would be in full gallop.

One of the riders bore down on them, his spurs deep in the girth of his mount. He drove the Black back toward the wall of the canyon, the others closing in from behind. Coming to an abrupt stop, the stallion twirled and headed north. Before he could gather speed, Alec heard the swish of a rope and saw the long, whirling loop fall over the head of his horse. He reached for it, but by the time his hands were on it, it had tightened. A few seconds later, the stallion was flung back on his haunches, throwing Alec to the ground.

He lay stunned for a few minutes, then he was jerked to his feet. Dazed, he looked around. The Black was held securely between the mounts of two men. The other horseman was standing in front of him, and Alec looked into the leering face of Ibn al Khaldun, who said softly, "Once again we meet, my young friend. Although I did not expect the pleasure so soon . . . nor here." His thick neck turned as he jerked his head over his shoulder. "Still, it is most unfortunate that you had to choose this time to visit me." He smiled, disclosing the toothless gums, then continued. "For now I must do away with you as well as the horse you call the Black. Most unfortunate . . . for you . . . that you, too, now stand in my way. It is a pity that one so young had to be so inquisitive." He sighed and his powerful chest rose and fell.

Alec was silent. This man was mad. He could not kill him! Or could he? Ibn al Khaldun was capable of anything, he knew. If he thought Alec stood in his way, he would murder him as easily as he had the others.

Ibn al Khaldun had him by the arm and his thick fingers dug deep, as he said, "You followed me from the meeting with Abu Já Kub ben Ishak, that much is obvious. Yes, I saw you there. But did you come alone? Perhaps your young friend accompanied you? The one who sat beside you on the roan. It is best that you speak now."

"You mean Abd-al-Rahman's brother?" Alec asked tauntingly, raising his head to meet the beady stare of the Bedouin. "No, I came alone." He grimaced in pain as Ibn al Khaldun's fingers tightened on his arm.

"$\hat{E}$ . . . yes, you know." The Bedouin smiled. "But in knowing you have answered my question. You overheard me talking to my men. You have seen too much, my young friend. And do you wish me to believe that in such a short time in our land you have learned Arabic so well you understood what I told my men? Obvious, is it not, that you were accompanied by another . . . by your young Bedouin friend?" Ibn al Khaldun smiled as he slowly twisted Alec's arm. "There are many other things still to be learned," he added, "if you will not tell me where he is hiding. Let me show you how simple it is for one who is strong enough to tear another's arm from its socket. This was shown to me when I was just a little older than you. It is the reason I have but one arm. Speak, my young friend, for we shall find him regardless, and it is not pleasant to lose an arm this way." His grip tightened and sharp, stabbing pains contorted Alec's face. Ibn al Khaldun's fingers loosened slightly. "It is odd," he said, "that once before I have sought information concerning the young brother of Abd-al-Rahman by this, shall we say, severe and, unfortunately, painful method. She was the nurse of the newborn son, whom we found alone in the desert many days after we had disposed of his father and mother. She, like you, would not tell us where she had left her young charge. Unfortunately, she died too soon for she was an old woman and could not stand much pain."

Ibn al Khaldun paused, then continued, "You are wondering how I recognized the brother of Abd-al-Rahman on the plain, are you not? I will tell you, although it will serve no purpose other than to show you that I am not without mercy." He paused again, and then went on, "In Haribwan several years ago, I saw a youth who resembled Abd-al-Rahman. And upon making inquiries I learned that which I had guessed to be true. This youth was his brother, for he had been found in the desert a few weeks after the time we had made our raid and, also, he bore the birthmark with which I, alone, was familiar . . . a small mole behind the lobe of the left ear. I decided that if he did not return to the desert I would leave him alone . . . for it was not necessary to do away with him so long as he was not recognized by those who knew his brother. But now that he is back, he will die . . . and we shall find him, my young friend, for he cannot escape us in this canyon."

With his free right hand, Alec swung and buried his fist in Ibn al Khaldun's fat stomach. The Bedouin winced and with lips drawn back twisted Alec's arm until his legs collapsed under him. He felt his strength going. The fall from the Black had weakened him. Bending, Ibn al Khaldun applied more pressure until everything began blotting out. Alec looked into the beady pig-eyes. Smiling, Ibn al Khaldun said hoarsely, "You will talk now, my young friend, or by Allah, I shall make you a present of your own arm!"

Alec was silent. He heard Ibn al Khaldun's voice, felt him breathing heavily on his neck. Everything was swimming about. His eyes, sunk deep in their sockets, rolled back. Vaguely, he made out the head of the Black, his long neck spotted with curds of white foam. Then he could see nothing.

He was suspended. It was light, then dark. Circles of revolving light sped through the heavens. He looked for the moon. Raj had said that when the moon rose above the mountains he would return with many men. He was being hunted. Somewhere in the darkness was Ibn al Khaldun. The Black knew and pulled at his bit. He wanted his head. Give it to him. He must get on. Time was passing, and things were happening. He struggled to get up, but was pushed back. The desert . . . the burning sand scorching his feet. Water! He had to have water. Raj had water . . . water from the chambers of the camel's stomach. He drank and it was good.

Alec opened his eyes. Overhead was the star-studded sky. Turning his head, he saw a figure holding a water canteen; behind him were two others and between them . . . the Black. Suddenly it all came back to him. Ibn al Khaldun! His arm . . . he turned his eyes to look for it. It was there but he could not raise it.

Ibn al Khaldun bent down and spoke to him. "It is a pity you cannot stand much pain," he whispered. "Yes, you still have your arm. I have wasted enough time on you and have thought of a better, a more appropriate way for you to die . . . one which will leave no evidence of, shall we say, foul play?'' He grasped Alec by the arm and roughly pulled him to his feet.

At first Alec could not stand by himself, and leaned heavily upon Ibn al Khaldun. Then, slowly, strength began returning to his limbs. He was dragged over to the mounted Bedouins and there boosted onto the back of the Black. The stallion shook his head furiously, trying to free it from the grip of the mounted horsemen, but their hands were strong and the rope tight.

Ibn al Khaldun mounted his horse, then said, ''This love you have for Shêtân has brought you many thousands of miles; now it is only fitting that you should accompany him in death.''

Alec grasped the Black's mane with his good hand; the other arm hung limply at his side. His head was clearing in the cool night air. Silently, he looked at Ibn al Khaldun's evil face. What did he intend to do?

''You are wondering, aren't you?'' Ibn al Khaldun asked. ''It is simple and you are fortunate, for death will be quick. It is a pity that I can't take longer, but it will, I suppose, take a little time to find your friend in the canyon, and all must be done before morning for we have other work then.'' He paused and grinned. ''Just a short distance up the canyon there is a cliff with a perpendicular drop of three hundred feet or so to the rocks below. You and your Black shall be driven over it. It is a pleasant way to die, is it not? The two of you inseparable even in death?''

He turned to his men, spoke tersely in Arabic, and then led the way up the canyon.

They moved slowly, for the mounts of the Bedouins

were terrified of the Black, and only the sharp spurs dug deep in their girths kept them going.

Alec's body was tense, his head cool. Astride the Black, confidence and new strength were flowing back into his tired body. There had to be some way out. He and the Black were not going to die as Ibn al Khaldun planned! His injured arm tingled as the blood again began circulating through it. Moving it slightly, he smiled grimly. Ibn al Khaldun would pay and pay well. He turned in his saddle toward the mountains in the rear. There was a slight glow and he knew that soon the moon would rise above them. If only he had more time!

Alec rubbed his legs gently but firmly along the stallion's girth. Snorting, the Black reared, pulling the startled Bedouins out of their saddles, their mounts screaming. Ibn al Khaldun, swearing and shouting to his men, drove his horse in on the Black. His mount shrilled painfully as the stallion's forelegs tore into him.

For a moment, as Ibn al Khaldun's mount staggered back under the weight of the stallion's hoofs, Alec thought the Black would break free. Then the Bedouins, fearing the fury of their leader more than they did the violent stallion, spurred their terrified mounts close to the Black until they again had him under control.

Enraged, Ibn al Khaldun glared and swore at Alec, then ordered his men to proceed.

They had not gone far when Ibn al Khaldun dropped back behind Alec. Tersely he gave orders to his men, and then said to Alec, "Ahead lies eternity, my young friend."

In the dim light, Alec could see the cliff which came to an abrupt drop about fifty yards beyond. And behind

Ibn al Khaldun the moon appeared above the rim of the mountains.

The Bedouins pressed their mounts closer to the Black. Ibn al Khaldun moved in from behind. Slowly the stallion was maneuvered toward the cliff.

Alec, his eyes on his horse's head, heard Ibn al Khaldun say, "The time has come to pray to your God, my friend. It is but a matter of seconds."

The sweating bodies of the Bedouins and their horses pressed closer; long, heavy crops dangled from the men's wrists. Alec knew that in just a second . . . a few more yards . . . they would bring their whips down upon the hindquarters of the Black and beat him until they drove him over the cliff.

He had to think fast.

Another few yards. Alec watched the hands of the Bedouins upon the rope around the stallion's neck. When they grabbed their crops there would be a fraction of a second in which only the pressure of their horses would hold the Black before they struck. It was then that he would have to act. It was his one chance of breaking free. The black mane was wet with perspiration from his clammy hands, his mouth dry and fuzzy.

The men's hands were still on the rope when there was a dull thud of leather biting deep into flesh. Screaming in pain, the Black bolted forward. Ibn al Khaldun had struck first!

Revenge

15

As the Black bolted forward, the Bedouins holding his head released their grips on the rope, grabbed their crops, and brought them down on the stallion.

Screaming in rage, the Black suddenly turned upon the horse to his left and descended upon it, his forelegs striking unmercifully. Alec clung like a burr to the great mane, as the Bedouin's horse went down under the hoofs of the Black, his rider pinned beneath him. Up and down the giant stallion pounded his forelegs into the pulpy mass of flesh at his feet. Desperately, Alec tried to pull him away but could not. The Black was again a savage, ruthless killer.

Alec turned his head and saw Ibn al Khaldun; in his hand was a gun. Unsteadily, he pointed it at the Black. He cursed as his mount, crazed by the smell of blood, lurched, almost throwing him from the saddle.

Suddenly the canyon echoed with the sharp cracks of

rifle fire. It rolled up the canyon in an ever increasing crescendo. Alec saw the moon high above the mountains. Raj and the warriors of Abu Já Kub ben Ishak and Abd-al-Rahman had arrived! His gaze swept back to Ibn al Khaldun. Startled, the Bedouin had turned in his saddle toward the lower canyon.

And now the Black stood still, his nostrils quivering and his ears cocked.

Alec knew that his was his chance to get away. Burying his head in the stallion's mane and sliding low on the huge body, he touched him with his heels.

The Black, as though released from a giant spring, swept past Ibn al Khaldun. Alec saw him jerk his head toward them, then raise his gun. His legs firm against the stallion's girth, he bent low. A few seconds later a bullet screamed above his head, then another. Alec jerked the Black's head and he swerved abruptly to the left. Ibn al Khaldun's next shot was wild. There were no others.

They had not gone far when the firing suddenly ceased, and silence filled the canyon. In long, powerful strides, the Black swept over the ground, his hoofs clattering against the stones. Alec attempted to calm him by talking into the cocked ears and rubbing his hand down the long, slender neck.

They were not far from the village when Alec heard the shouts of men, their voices raised high in anger. The speed of the Black slackened and Alec peered into the darkness ahead. Gradually, the huts took shape.

When he arrived at the end of the long street, the shouting had stopped. He brought the Black to a walk, and slowly they passed the first of the huts.

He had not gone far when the figures of many men loomed in the night. Alec approached cautiously, not knowing what lay ahead. Crab-stepping, the Black whistled softly. The answering neighs of many horses filled the air. Alec brought the stallion to a halt.

A horseman approached, and Alec recognized the gray stallion of Abu Já Kub ben Ishak. He called out, fearing that the sheikh would take him for one of Ibn al Khaldun's men. Spurring the gray, Abu Ishak rode up to Alec. His stern face relaxed as he recognized Alec and Shêtân. "It is well you are safe, Alec," he said. "When we did not find you we were worried." His features clouded. "Ibn al Khaldun is not among those we have captured. Have you seen him?"

Hastily, Alec told him what had happened, and when he had finished Abu Já Kub ben Ishak spun his gray around on its haunches. "Come," he said.

Alec followed him back to his men, who astride their horses encircled Ibn al Khaldun's defeated warriors. Sullenly, they stood within the circle.

Abd-al-Rahman rode up to Abu Já Kub ben Ishak, his chestnut stallion rearing at the sight of the Black. The older sheikh motioned Alec away.

Raj suddenly appeared upon his roan. "Alec," he said, "are you all right?"

"Sure, Raj . . . I'm okay. But you arrived just in time." Then Alec told him what had happened, and that Ibn al Khaldun was somewhere up the canyon.

"They will capture him before morning," Raj said, when Alec had finished. "$\hat{E}$ . . . yes, some of the men go now!"

A large group of men, their rifles held high in the air,

drove their mounts up the canyon behind Abd-al-Rahman.

Raj whirled his roan and rode up to Abu Já Kub ben Ishak. Alec followed.

"My brother . . . he goes in search of Ibn al Khaldun." Raj's voice was tense as he spoke to Abu Já Kub ben Ishak. "Did he not want me to ride with him?"

"He thought it best that you stay with me," the sheikh said. "We will take these men back to your brother's home and there await him . . . and Ibn al Khaldun." Abu Já Kub ben Ishak turned to Alec. The stallion shook his head as Alec rubbed him behind the ears. Smiling, the sheikh said, "It is now easy for me to believe what I have heard about you and Shêtân." He paused, then continued, "I would like to have you take him home. Some of my men will accompany you, so you have no need to fear."

Alec nodded. "As you wish, sir," he replied, ". . . but I would prefer to go along with you and Raj."

"It is better that you go," the sheikh insisted. His gaze shifted to Ibn al Khaldun's men and he added, "That which lies ahead is not pleasant. They will be given the opportunity to speak for themselves, but they are murderers, outlaws all . . . and will be dealt with accordingly." He stopped and then his eyes returned to Alec and Raj. "Come, let us be on our way."

A short time later the long line of men rode down the canyon; behind them the bright flames of burning huts reached high into the blackened sky.

It was three days later that Alec, astride the Black, and the small group of men Abu Já Kub ben Ishak had sent with him, traveled up the ravine to the narrow chasm which opened into the valley. Bending forward in his saddle, Alec wiped the white lather from the glistening neck of the Black. They had traveled fast these last three days, for the men were anxious to get back to their families. As for himself, he looked forward to seeing Henry and Mr. Volence again . . . yes, and Tabari, too . . . for he felt she would be more than interested to learn that the feud between her father and Abd-al-Rahman was over.

They entered the darkened chasm and a few minutes later emerged upon the trail overlooking the valley. Playing with his bit, the Black pranced nervously, his eyes scanning the floor below. His ears pricked suddenly forward as he spied a small lone group of running colts at the upper end. Then he screamed, and his wild, shrill whistle echoed throughout the valley.

Alec saw the running horses come to an abrupt halt. The Black screamed again as they made their way down the trail. Bolting, the horses came galloping toward them.

When they reached the floor, the horses were but a few hundred yards away. They had stopped and were moving nervously around in small circles, their heads and ears cocked in the direction of the Black.

Spurring their horses, the Bedouins set out for their homes at a gallop. Alec held the Black while he danced. For a moment he thrilled to the sensitive body and powerful muscles beneath him. A warm glow of confidence and pride flowed through his veins as the giant horse awaited his command.

When the others were well on their way down the

valley, Alec relaxed the pressure on his knees and gave the stallion his head. With giant strides the Black gained momentum rapidly. Ahead the colts broke and ran as the stallion descended upon them. Reaching the stragglers, the Black ran close and shrilled loudly. Then with ever increasing speed he ran the others down. Reaching the colts in front, his speed slackened until they drew ahead, then, spurting, he would pass them with blinding speed only to slow down again.

Alec reveled in the tremendous speed of the stallion, as the heavy black mane flew back in his face and his eyes watered from the wind. It had been a long time since he had had the opportunity of doing this.

In a sudden burst of speed, the Black drew rapidly away from the colts. Alec crouched low against the stallion's neck. Ahead, near the home of Abu Já Kub ben Ishak, he saw Tabari and, standing beside her, the white filly, Jôhar.

As he neared them, Alec took back on the reins. The Black fought and then slowly relented, slackening his speed.

Tabari looked at Alec anxiously when he brought the Black to a stop before her. "Why have you returned with so few men?" she asked him in a strained voice. "My father. Where is he? What has happened?"

Alec smiled, dispelling her fears. "Everything is all right, Tabari," he said, dismounting and rubbing a hand across his face. He grabbed the reins and flung them over the stallion's head, allowing him to go over to Jôhar. Then he turned to Tabari. "Nothing is wrong. Your father will be home within a few days. I have a lot to tell you, but first I must take care of my horse. He's had a hard ride."

"You found him then at Abd-al-Rahman's?" Tabari asked, her eyes saddening.

"No, Tabari," Alec replied. "Abd-al-Rahman didn't steal him. He is now your father's friend rather than his enemy. But I'd rather tell you the whole story from the beginning. Call Henry and Mr. Volence and I'll meet you in the library in a few minutes, when I return from the stables."

As Alec led the Black away, Tabari said, "The men at the stables . . . they will take care of him, Alec."

"I'd rather do it, Tabari."

Understandingly, the girl nodded and walked quickly toward the house.

Plain of Andulla

16

That evening after dinner Henry, Mr. Volence, Tabari and Alec walked out on the long veranda. It seemed to Alec that Tabari's eyes shone as they never had before. Her full lips parted as she said, with a smile, ''You probably have much to talk over with Alec, so I'll leave you alone.'' Without waiting for them to reply, she turned and walked down the steps.

Alec was wondering if it was not she who wanted to be alone, when Henry said, ''Boy, you sure get into things, don't you?''

''It's okay''—Alec laughed—''so long as I can get out of them after I'm in. Luck's been with me so far.''

Mr. Volence's face was somber. ''It's fortunate that you're young, Alec,'' he said quietly, ''and can laugh at things like that. Pretty serious business, though, and I'm thankful to God you came through it. Your arm . . . you're sure it's coming along all right?''

"Yes," Alec said, raising his injured arm, "a few more days and it'll be as good as ever."

Henry sat on the railing. "Do you think they'll have much trouble runnin' down Ibn al Khaldun?" he asked.

Alec's voice was solemn. "I hope not, Henry . . . but he's a slippery guy and treacherous, as we all know. Still, he'll have to move fast to get away from Abd-al-Rahman and his men." Alec withdrew the gold chain and medallion from his pocket and studied the figure of the large bird.

"Then it is the Phoenix," Mr. Volence said quietly.

"Yes," Alec replied. "It was their symbol . . . for like the Phoenix, Ibn al Khaldun hoped to rise to power."

"But to destroy and kill," muttered Henry.

They sat silently in the darkness of the veranda. After several minutes Mr. Volence said, "I don't suppose Raj will return to Haribwan."

"No, I'm certain he won't," Alec replied. "He'll want to stay with his brother."

"Funny world," growled Henry. "Wait'll we tell Mr. Coggins that his houseboy turned out to be Abd-al-Rahman's brother."

Alec looked at them anxiously. "You two sound as though we'll be leaving before long," he said.

Smiling, Mr. Volence said, "Not until after the race, anyway, Alec."

"Tabari told us she was certain her father'd see to it that we got back okay," Henry informed Alec. He paused to light his pipe, then added, "If the Black wins maybe Abu Ishak will let us have a couple of horses, as Tabari told you, remember?"

"Yes, I remember," Alec nodded. "How long before the race?" His gaze turned to the moon which hung low over the valley. It was in the last quarter, and the day of the new moon was not far off.

Henry's voice came to him. "Three days from tomorrow, according to Tabari."

Alec looked fixedly at Henry. "But what if Abu Ishak doesn't return in time . . . and Abd-al-Rahman . . . there's no telling where his chase of Ibn al Khaldun will lead, or how long it'll take."

"We mentioned that same thing to her tonight after dinner," Henry said, looking at Mr. Volence; then turning to Alec he added, "She said neither of 'em would miss the race . . . seemed pretty positive about it, too."

Alec sat down on the railing beside Henry. He was silent a moment and then he looked up at Mr. Volence, whom he found watching him. Alec's eyes turned to Henry; his eyes, too, were upon him. His gaze shifted from one to the other, then coming to rest upon Mr. Volence he asked, "Had you thought about Abu Ishak not having a rider for the race?"

Mr. Volence nodded. "Yes," he said quietly, "we had thought about it."

"Do you think," Alec asked, "there's any chance of my riding?"

Henry rose from the railing. "We were gonna ask you that, Alec." He paused. "Abu Ishak let you ride the

Black back home, didn't he? And it was you who got him away from Ibn al Khaldun. Seems to me he'd let you ride. After all, he's in a spot, isn't he? Who else can ride that black devil, anyway?"

Alec's head reeled at the thought of being able to ride his horse in the race against Sagr. Never in the world would there be anything to equal it. His eager eyes met Henry's. "Maybe, Henry," he said, ". . . maybe."

Two days later Abu Já Kub ben Ishak returned with his men. He dismounted from his gray and made his way toward the house. Alec noticed that his face was grave. Tabari threw her arms around him and his taut face relaxed for a moment, then sobered again as he greeted them.

"Was Ibn al Khaldun captured?" Alec asked.

Abu Já Kub ben Ishak shook his head. "Abd-al-Rahman returned without him. . . . His men were still searching when I left, but they, too, will return in time for the race. When it is finished we will set out again and by Allah the sun will not set until we have found him."

". . . and the others? His men?" Alec asked.

"It is over for them," Abu Ishak replied briefly. Then, turning, he walked into the house.

An hour later Alec was summoned to Abu Ishak's bedroom. When he entered, the sheikh, who was sitting in a large chair by the window, turned toward him and said, "Come in, Alec. I wish to talk with you." He motioned toward the chair opposite him.

Alec sat down and waited for Abu Ishak to speak. Thoughtfully, the sheikh gazed out of the window, then without looking at Alec he said softy, "I would like to know, Alec, if you would consent to ride Shêtân in the race the day after tomorrow."

The blood rushed to Alec's face as he leaped from his chair. "G-Gosh! I sure would, sir! It's what I've been hoping for all along!" He stood over the sheikh, his voice high with unrestrained emotion.

Abu Já Kub ben Ishak smiled as he looked at Alec, then his face sobered. "It will not be an easy ride," he said. "The best horses in Arabia will be entered, and the men riding them will be the finest of our horsemen."

Alec nodded and sat down again in his chair. "Who will be up on Sagr?" he asked.

"Abd-al-Rahman, for no other has ever ridden him." He paused, then added, "Shêtân must be at his best to win . . . of that much I am certain, for I know the speed and endurance of Sagr."

"What is the distance of the race?" Alec asked. His face had lost its boyishness, and an intense seriousness was written on his countenance. He had complete confidence in the Black, but in a race such as this many things could happen.

"The course is four miles," Abu Já Kub ben Ishak told him.

"And the terrain?" Alec asked.

"It varies," the sheikh said, "from grass-swept plains to the desert, from rocky mountainous trails to brush-covered flats. The course was laid out by our people to test the courage and hearts of our horses, not speed and endurance alone."

Alec remained silent when Abu Já Kub ben Ishak had

finished. Finally, he said confidently, "The Black, Shêtân, has the heart."

The sheikh nodded. "Yes, I think he has, Alec . . . it has been bred into him, and I do not think he will disappoint us." He rose from his chair and walked to the window. "My people feast tonight in celebration of the coming race. They have great faith in Shêtân, and much will be wagered with other tribesmen. We must not fail them, as we have in other races." He turned to Alec. "We will leave tomorrow morning, and before sundown will arrive at the Plain of Andulla where the race takes place. Your friends will be eager to go, so please tell them to be ready."

Sleep did not come soon to Alec that night. Wide awake, he lay in bed listening to the voices of the Bedouins raised high in song and laughter as they feasted. He thought of what winning the race meant to them and to Abu Já Kub ben Ishak. A smile crossed his face as he remembered Henry's words when he had told them he was going to ride the Black in the race . . . "Glory be, Alec, you're the luckiest kid ever to put foot in a stirrup!"

But Mr. Volence had not shared Henry's enthusiasm. "I know it's what you wanted, Alec," he had said, his face grave and drawn with concern, "but I wish you weren't riding. Handling the Black is a big job in itself, and in a race such as this there's no telling what he'll do. The terrain is another thing to consider. The Bedouins know it well, probably every inch of it, while it will be new to you. They will watch you closely for they fear Shêtân, and if you make the slightest mistake, I'm sure they will move to their advantage. You are not in America, Alec, and don't forget it for a second. . . . In this race there will be no rules.''

Alec turned on his side. He realized well the dangers ahead, the responsibility he would assume once he mounted the Black. Nor did he underestimate the speed, heart and stamina of the other horses and the skill of their riders. But he had confidence in his horse . . . confidence in himself. And, like Henry, he felt that he was the luckiest kid ever to put foot in a stirrup. A few minutes later his eyes closed and he slept.

The long line of horsemen extended halfway down the floor of the valley. In front rode Abu Já Kub ben Ishak on his gray stallion. Beside him, straight and slim in her saddle, sat Tabari on Jôhar. Alec, astride a bay horse and leading the Black, rode behind him, followed by Henry, Mr. Volence and Abu Ishak's tribesmen and their families.

Alec turned in his saddle and looked at the line trailing far behind them. They were all there . . . the men, the women, even the children; those old enough to hold a rein rode their own ponies, the others were lightly held in their fathers' arms. Colorful trappings draped the saddles and bridles of their horses. Some of the men carried spears and vari-colored shields. They laughed and shouted as their horses trotted along.

They rode easily thoughout the day, the well-traveled trail which they were following taking them to the west in the direction of the desert.

It was still light when Tabari, turning in her saddle, called to Alec, "Ahead is the Plain of Andulla." Alec saw the broad, brush-covered plain before them, topping a rise in the ground. Long lines of colorful caravans like their own moved across it toward the west, where the plain merged with the white sands of the desert. A wave of excitement passed through Alec and swept down the line to the men, women and children of Abu Já Kub ben Ishak's tribe. "We're here!" whispered Alec, as his bay horse moved to a fast trot to keep up with others. The Black ran easily beside him, his ears pricked.

The traffic became heavier as they converged with other caravans on the plain. Clouds of gray dust rose from beneath the hoofs of dancing horses. Some Bedouins were on foot, their voices raised high in songs and chants as they stamped the ground. One group capered alongside Alec. An old Bedouin with wrinkled face studied the Black, then his brown, flickering eyes under half-closed eyelids turned to Alec. "Shêtân? Shêtân?" he asked in a high crackling voice.

Alec nodded. The Bedouin stamped his feet until the gray dust all but obliterated his thin figure. He screeched loudly to the others in his group and they ran quickly toward Alec and the Black. However, before they reached the stallion, several of Abu Já Kub ben Ishak's men rode in among them to keep them from getting too close. Their cries pierced the air as they ran alongside the horses. Finally, as Abu Já Kub ben Ishak increased the pace of his horsemen, they dropped behind.

After a short time they came to the main camp on the

edge of the desert. Men, women, boys and girls by the thousands were already there. Some were busily pitching their tents, others were standing around their cooking fires . . . all were excitedly awaiting the coming race.

Abu Já Kub ben Ishak led his band away from the others, and as they passed the many groups there came the shrill cries of "Shêtân! . . . Shêtân!"

Alec's blood pounded as he heard them shout and turn eager eyes toward his horse. He marveled at the calmness of Abu Já Kub ben Ishak and Tabari, who rode ahead. A stranger among these people, Alec felt closer to the Black than ever before. He leaned from his saddle and reached out to pat the stallion. What, he wondered, would be the outcome of tomorrow's race?

The Race

17

Alec awakened the next day to find that many more tribes had come in during the night. He saw the Bedouins standing by their cooking fires, their voices raised high and shrill. There was a tenseness in the air, and already many were squatting and standing around the space where the race would start. Alec felt keyed up. . . . He was anxious for the race to begin.

Smiling, he shook his head as one of Abu Já Kub ben Ishak's servants offered him breakfast. He did not feel like eating. A large group was clustered about the Black and he made his way toward them.

Abu Já Kub ben Ishak saw Alec and strode up. "It will not be long now," he said. "We race before the sun becomes too hot."

"I'm all set," Alec told him. "How about the Black? Is he all right?"

"Yes . . . my men are keeping the others away from him. He is excited but that is to be expected." He paused, then added, "Ride Shêtân as you see fit, Alec. I have no instructions . . . only, remember that the men who ride against you know the terrain well. For that reason it is better that you do not set the pace. You have studied the map of the course which I gave you last night?"

Alec nodded. "I know it," he said. It was clear in his mind just how he would ride this race. In the broken mountainous country the others would have the advantage for, as Abu Já Kub ben Ishak had said, they knew the terrain and were used to it. He would keep the Black close to the leaders until they reached the open country. . . . Then, across the desert to the brush-covered plain, would come the test. He felt confident that the Black would pick up the lost ground when he called upon him.

The soft rhythmic beating of drums suddenly resounded across the plain, stilling the voices of the Bedouins. Then the men began to dance while women and girls clapped their hands and chanted. Shouting, whistling, and hissing through their teeth the men stamped their feet upon the ground, the dust rising in soft whirls about their bodies.

"Come," Abu Já Kub ben Ishak said, "it is almost time."

Alec followed him as the sheikh walked toward the group still clustered about the Black. They fell away, forming a narrow path as Abu Já Kub ben Ishak reached them. Alec felt their curious eyes upon him as he walked up to the black stallion, who was already wearing bridle and saddle.

Running his hand across the stallion's neck, Alec pulled the small head to him. The Black nuzzled him with mole-soft lips.

Pushing their way through the crowd, Henry and Mr. Volence entered the circle. "We've been lookin' over the others," Henry said. "They're the finest bunch o' horseflesh I've ever set eyes on."

Mr. Volence nodded in agreement. "They are, Alec," he said. "You'll have to get everything out of the Black today."

"I will," Alec said confidently.

The shouting of the dancing Bedouins and the booming of the drums rose to a new, high pitch. Abu Já Kub ben Ishak touched Alec on the shoulder. "It is time," he said in a low voice.

Nodding in assent, Alec drew off his head shawl and then stripped to the waist. Finishing, he turned to the sheikh. "Okay, sir, I'm ready," he said.

Henry moved alongside him. "Let me boost you up for good luck, Alec," he offered.

Smiling, Alec pushed his knee into Henry's lowered hands. The Black pranced nervously as soon as he was in the saddle. Quieting him, Alec caught Henry's eye and a look of understanding passed between them. Henry lifted Alec's feet out of the long stirrups and shortened them until his knees rested high on the stallion's withers. The saddle had been weighted to make up for Alec's light body, and now the Black carried no less than any other horse in the race.

The white-robed Bedouins standing in a circle around them looked at one another and then conversed in lowered tones. How strange, they were saying, that astride Shêtân, the stallion of Sheikh Abu Já Kub ben Ishak, should sit this unrobed white-skinned youth who rode with such short stirrups. Ê, by Allah, the Sheikh Abu Já Kub ben Ishak must have lost his head! What chance had Shêtân now against a great stallion like Sagr with the Sheikh Abd-al-Rahman's long, powerful limbs pressed about his girth? Dispersing, they ran to seek the tribesmen of Abu Já Kub ben Ishak whose misguided loyalty would prompt them to wager on Shêtân.

Abu Já Kub ben Ishak, his hand on Shêtân's halter, pointed toward a tent set apart from the others, and Alec saw an old man squatting in the shade.

"That is the Sheikh Abdullah ben Brehim. He has seen more races than any of us, and was a great friend of my father. It is he who will start the race and declare the winner."

Alec watched as the old man rose to his feet and with short strides walked past them. He was not more than five feet tall and his face was wrinkled with age. A red shawl covered his head and matched the flowing garment he wore over his slight body. A short way beyond them he raised a thin hand and the chanting and dancing of the Bedouins stopped. Silence reigned across the Plain of Andulla as he strode toward the starting place.

They waited until the old sheikh had squatted upon the ground, then Abu Já Kub ben Ishak turned to Alec. "Come . . . he is ready," he said. Leading the Black, they went toward the starting line. Ahead of them swarmed the Bedouins, forming a line on both sides of the place where the race would start.

Tossing his head, the Black kept reaching for his bit, and his ears cocked quickly as he saw the other horses and riders approaching the starting line. Alec counted five of them; the nearest to him was Sagr, his golden mane shining in the early morning sun. He crab-stepped nervously when he saw the Black. Astride him Abd-al-Rahman smiled and lifted his crop; then his legs tightened about Sagr's girth and he moved ahead down the long passage lined with cheering spectators.

"That is a horse," said Abu Já Kub ben Ishak, turning to Alec. "There will never be a race to equal this one." Removing his hand from the stallion's bridle, he added, "Go now, Alec, for the rest is up to you and Shêtân."

Turning in his saddle, Alec waved at Henry and Mr. Volence, who were walking behind him. Then he shortened his reins and moved forward in the saddle. Halfway to the starting line, Alec heard his name called and turning, saw Raj.

"I wish you much luck, Alec," Raj said, running alongside.

"Even with your brother and Sagr in the race?" Alec smiled.

"$\hat{E}$ . . . yes, for I have a wager with him that your Black will beat Sagr." Raj's eyes turned toward the starting line. "They are waiting to begin, Alec." He waved and left.

As they neared the other horses, Alec felt the Black's giant body quiver between his legs. Then the stallion's wild, shrill whistle shattered the air, silencing the voices of the Bedouins. Eyes turned toward them, and the other horses moved uneasily, their teeth bared beneath curled nostrils.

The old sheikh on the starting line rose to his feet and motioned Alec forward. As the Black approached, Sagr reared and fought for his head. Abd-al-Rahman pulled him down, and moved a short distance away.

Alec held a light but firm hand on the reins. Rising in his stirrups, he patted the Black's neck and talked to him. Turning back an ear, the stallion listened and was quiet.

Abdullah ben Brehim raised his hand when the Black reached the starting line, and turning his dry, wrinkled face up to Alec, he smiled. Then his gaze passed down the line to see if the others were ready.

A tenseness gripped Alec's body and unconsciously he drew back on the reins. Snorting, the stallion plunged over the line. Alec pulled him to a stop and then, turning, made his way back amidst the taunts and laughter of the spectators. He did not mind their laughing. Catching sight of the flashing brown eyes of Abd-al-Rahman, he smiled. The sheikh raised his crop and the pressure of his legs made Sagr rear, his forelegs pawing the air.

Alec again lined the Black up with the others. The tenseness had left his body and he felt calm and confident. He glanced quickly down the line at the taut faces of the men as they sat lightly on their horses, which had been born and bred for just this race. All possessed bodies of wonderful physical perfection . . . slanting shoulders, deep broad chests, powerful legs and knees not too high nor too low, all marks of speed and endurance. Yes, as Abu Já Kub ben Ishak had said, this would be a race . . . and never would there be another to equal it!

Alec leaned forward in his saddle. Between the pricked ears of the Black he could see the little old sheikh in the red headdress and gown, his hand still raised high in the air, his half-closed eyes still upon them. The spectators were silent; only the hoofs of the horses moving restlessly in place broke the stillness. Perspiration rolled from Alec's face and neck and trickled down his back. He pressed his knees hard into the stallion's black body. Any second now. The Black sensed it from the pressure of Alec's knees. He stopped prancing, his ears pitched forward. Then the arm of the old man dropped.

The horses shot forward as one. Alec heard the shouts of the Bedouins as the Black bolted. Then he could hear nothing but the pounding of hoofs; feel nothing but the surge of great muscles between his legs; see nothing but the ground slipping away in long, rolling waves beneath him.

Sagr, faster at the break, took the lead. Alec, content to let Abd-al-Rahman set the pace, moved the Black over beside the chestnut stallion and held his nose even with the other's stirrups. Galloping well, the Black fought for his head. Alec held the reins firm and talked to him. Glancing over his shoulder, he saw the others riding hard a few yards behind.

In front the course lay open. So far everything had gone as he'd planned. He would cling to Sagr's heels across the brush-covered flat and into the mountains. Then as they entered the last half of the race, which would take them over the desert and back to the starting place, he would call upon the Black . . . and he was certain the great stallion would not fail him.

The Black had hold of his bit, but was not pulling. As he galloped across the plain, swirls of gray dust rose behind them. Abd-al-Rahman, his long black beard whipping in the wind, glanced back as they neared the trail that would lead them through the mountains. Then he sat down to ride, and Sagr leaped forward.

Alec loosened the reins slightly and kept close behind him. Sagr's powerful quarters rose and fell in front and Abd-al-Rahman's back and shoulders swayed as he swung with him.

They turned into the mountainous trail without slackening their speed. It was a gradual ascent lined with overhanging brush that tore at Alec's bare flesh. Turning slightly in his saddle, he saw that the others had slowed down, sparing their mounts. Ahead Sagr was galloping as though it were the finish and Alec wondered whether he could possibly keep up this speed. For a second he drew back on the reins and the Black fought for his head. Sagr increased his lead and thundered ahead.

Finally the trail leveled and they entered a long ravine with towering cliffs on each side. Sagr's powerful quarters rose and fell fifty yards away. Alec moved far forward in his saddle and gave the Black his head. As the stallion extended himself, his feet scarcely touched the ground and he slowly cut down Sagr's lead. Alec saw Abd-al-Rahman glance behind at the sound of the Black's thundering hoofs. Reaching for his crop, he moved it alongside the chestnut and he sprang forward.

Alec was certain now that it was Abd-al-Rahman's intention to run the others into the ground early in the race. And with the exception of the Black he was doing it, for the two were far in the lead. Alec wondered whether his horse could keep up with Sagr. The Black was galloping hard, and lather ran from his body.

The trail led up again at the end of the ravine, and Alec felt the Black gather himself and the surge of great muscles. He raised his hands and, responding, the stallion galloped up the trail.

Sweat ran from Alec's body and painfully entered the open cuts he had suffered from the brush. Sagr was just ahead and Alec could hear the heaving of his body. They neared the top and Alec knew they had covered half the distance. Two more miles to go. He moved farther forward on the stallion's neck and placed a hand on the wet coat.

Abd-al-Rahman's swaying body disappeared from view as Sagr reached the summit. Alec knew that the trail would now lead down a short distance to the desert. It would be then that he would have to call upon the Black for every last bit of speed and stamina he had in his giant body.

As he reached the summit, he saw Sagr halfway across the open flat which led down to the desert. Suddenly there was the sharp crack of a gun and the dirt kicked up in front of Sagr! Alec pulled hard on the Black, slackening his speed. There was another shot! It came from the brush to the right of the flat, and Alec, turning quickly in his saddle, saw the outline of a man's body. *Ibn al Khaldun!* Alec turned the stallion and bore down upon him.

The white-robed firgure, intent upon bringing Abd-al-Rahman in his gun sights, did not see Alec until the black stallion was a short distance away from him. Then Ibn al Khaldun turned, fear showing in his swarthy face as the stallion swept toward him. Screaming, the Black reared with Alec clinging to his neck. Ibn al Khaldun stumbled on the brush and fell to the ground. Rolling quickly, he turned and pointed his pistol at the Black, who rose high above him with pawing hoofs. His pupils were dilated and blood and sweat ran down the fatty crevices of his face as his finger tightened on the trigger of his wavering gun. Alec jerked the stallion's head, attempting to pull him to one side. Then the crack of a gun shattered the air.

The Black did not shudder. There had been no impact of bullet against flesh. Alec would have felt it had the bullet struck its mark! But how could Ibn al Khaldun have missed at this close range? The powerful forelegs of the stallion descended and struck the ground, close to the body of the Bedouin, who lay flat on his back, his arm outstretched and fingers still clasped on the butt of his gun. A dark red blotch spread slowly over his heart and his beady eyes were rolled back. Alec knew he was dead.

The Black struck at the prone body, the scent of Ibn al Khaldun strong in his nostrils. Pulling him away, Alec heard the sound of hoofs behind. Abd-al-Rhaman rode up, gun in hand, and Alec realized it had been his gun he had heard and not Ibn al Khaldun's.

Without a word, Abd-al-Rahman jumped off Sagr's sweating body and went to Ibn al Khaldun. He bent down over him a minute, then straightened and looked at Alec. Perspiration poured from his face and his black beard was wet. He said something in Arabic, then casting Ibn al Khaldun's gun aside, he mounted Sagr. His gaze turned to the trail over which they had come. The ring of many hoofs against stone came to their ears. Nodding to Alec, Abd-al-Rahman raised his crop and then wheeled Sagr in a swirl of red dust.

Alec glanced at the lifeless body of Ibn al Khaldun and the fat face which was even more hideous and evil in death. The unwritten law of the desert had been enforced. The deaths of the mother and father of Abd-al-Rahman had been avenged by their son. Alec wheeled the Black and set out after Sagr.

He held the stallion back as they swept down the trail toward the desert which stretched out below them. He noticed that Abd-al-Rahman was now also saving Sagr for the race to come on the flat. The Bedouin sheikh glanced back more often, and Alec knew he wondered how much speed and stamina the Black had left. He had staked much on tiring him before they reached the desert. Alec smiled and was confident, for the Black was running well and pulling at his bit. It was a good sign.

Sagr had reached the desert and Abd-al-Rahman sat down to ride. Alec knew that he would not glance back again for there was but a mile and a half to go and he would drive Sagr hard to the finish.

The Black left the trail and pounded onto the desert. Stumbling as his hoofs sank into the sand, he recovered and drove forward. Alec moved forward in his saddle and gave the stallion his head. The Black extended his body and with long strides swept over the sand, scarcely touching the ground. Sixty yards ahead thundered Sagr, the white sand flying from beneath his hoofs.

The course led up the edge of the desert, the mountains rising high on the right, and nothing but the broad expanse of white burning sand to the left. Far ahead Alec could see the mountains as they descended to the Plain of Andulla over which they would ride to the finish.

A mile to go and the distance between Sagr and the Black had lessened. Abd-al-Rahman was using his crop lightly.

Alec had not yet called upon the Black for everything. He was content to let Abd-al-Rahman keep his lead until they entered the homestretch across the plain. The footing would be better on the hard ground.

As they swept onto the plain Abd-al-Rahman began using his whip, and under it Sagr pulled ahead again until twenty yards separated him from the Black. The finish was near now and a quarter of a mile ahead Alec could see the Bedouins swarming around the finish line. Moving forward in his saddle, he raised his hands and call upon the Black. "C'mon, fella," he shouted into the leveled ears. "C'mon!"

Slowly, the giant stallion cut the lead. Slowly, he moved up behind Sagr. Powerful muscles heaved as the two horses extended themselves. Stride for stride they moved forward; and inch by inch the Black gained.

To one side Bedouins galloped, shouting and firing their guns. Several attempted to keep up with them, but even their fresh horses could not stand the swift pace and soon fell back.

Only two hundred yards to go. Alec could see the

colored dresses of the women and distinguished the red headdress and gown of the old sheikh as he stood alone and apart from the others at the finish line.

Already the people were opening a path for them to gallop through. Alec knew that the time had come. Leaning forward, he called again to the Black and slapped him with his open hand. The stallion drew alongside Sagr and they rode neck to neck, stirrup to stirrup. Neither horse showed any sign of faltering as they galloped stride for stride, their strained bodies glistening with sweat and powdered with gray dust.

Entering the path to the finish line, Alec saw Abd-al-Rahman glance toward him, then his crop fell heavily on the chestnut's flank. At the same time Alec slapped the Black's neck. Simultaneously, both horses shot forward as though hurled from a giant spring. Thundering, they pounded down to the finish line. So close to the Black's neck that his body was enveloped by the long flowing mane, Alec called upon his horse for the last time. Between his knees he felt the surge of powerful muscles as the Black extended himself. Slowly he inched ahead of Sagr until he was in front by a head . . . then a neck. As the Black forged ahead, Alec suddenly saw Sagr, his teeth bared, whip his head toward the Black's neck in an attempt to ravage him! Screaming in anger, the black stallion turned upon Sagr. Alec jerked his horse's head away from the chestnut, and as he did he saw Abd-al-Rahman lay his crop across Sagr's muzzle. As the Black sprang forward, increasing his lead, Abd-al-Rahman's eyes met Alec's for a fraction of a second; then he raised his crop in a salute as the Black swept over the finish line.

Conclusion

18

A week after the race Abd-al-Rahman came to the home of Abu Já Kub ben Ishak. With him he brought the fifteen horses which Abu Ishak had selected from his herd after the Black's victory. Raj, who accompanied him, told Alec, "My brother says that the Sheikh Abu Já Kub ben Ishak does not have faint eyesight when he looks for fine horses. He has taken the best of our stock." He paused and smiled. "It will be different, the next race. . . . There will be no Shêtân." Then he added admiringly, "That was a fine race you rode, Alec. My brother said that no Bedouin could have equaled it. He was very much impressed for he did not think you could handle the black stallion."

"He is all horse, Raj, and we have gotten to know one another well." Alec's voice was soft as he added, "I wouldn't be too sure about winning the next race. Abu

196

Já Kub ben Ishak will not sit idly through the next five years. No, Raj, the blood of the Black will be in the horse that Abu Ishak sends to the next race. You can be sure of that . . . and he, like the Black, will be hard to beat.''

Raj looked at Alec. ''It will be difficult for you to leave him behind, will it not?''

Alec nodded. ''But it is better . . . for he belongs here. I know that now.''

They walked to the porch of the big house in silence. Then Raj asked, ''Will Mr. Volence take any of Abu Ishak's horses back with him?''

''Yes, he has given him four.''

''Mr. Volence . . . he is pleased?''

''Very much,'' Alec replied, ''For they are four of Abu Ishak's finest, and much better than any he had hoped to find in Arabia. We're taking them with us tomorrow.''

''Tomorrow?'' Raj asked, his inquisitive brown eyes seeking those of his friend. ''But that is too soon. Can you not stay longer? We could have many good times together now that there is peace between my family and that of Abu Já Kub ben Ishak.'' His voice lowered to a whisper. ''Can you keep a secret, my friend? Ê . . . yes, you must, for if you do not and my brother hears of it, I fear he will send me back to Haribwan.''

''Sure, Raj. What is it?''

His friend's voice was so low Alec could scarcely hear him. ''There is to be a wedding,'' he whispered. ''My brother has asked the Sheikh Abu Já Kub ben Ishak for the hand of his daughter, Tabari, and he has given his consent. My brother spaks to Tabari today, if he has not already, and if she agrees to become his bride there will be much feasting and celebration among our people. Could you not stay for it, Alec?''

Alec shook his head and smiled. ''I'd like to, Raj, very much. But by starting tomorrow we'll arrive at Aden in time to meet a freighter which Abu Já Kub ben Ishak told us is scheduled to stop there in three weeks.'' He paused. ''I'm sure there will be a wedding for I saw your brother walking with Tabari a short while ago and she didn't look as though she would refuse him.''

Abu Já Kub ben Ishak, with Henry and Mr. Volence, walked toward them from the direction of the stables. When he reached the porch steps the sheikh asked Alec to come with him into the library. There, he shut the door behind him and said, ''I wish to have a few words with you, Alec, and would rather not have the others hear what I have to say.''

Alec sat down in the chair Abu Já Kub ben Ishak offered him. He watched the sheikh as he stood silently looking out of the long window. Finally, turning to Alec, he spoke. ''I need not tell you,'' he said, ''that I am very grateful. . . . That you know, I am certain. I know also of your great love for Shêtân, and his for you.'' He paused, then after a few seconds continued. ''It is not possible for me to give him to you, for to do that would be to throw away all the years of careful breeding that have been spent in the development of such a horse. And from Shêtân I must breed others.''

''I didn't expect you to give me the Black . . .'' Alec interrupted. ''I know how valuable he is to you. It isn't necessary for you to explain.'' He rose from his chair.

Abu Já Kub ben Ishak moved over to Alec and placed

a hand on his shoulder. "There is just one thing more, Alec," he said. "As you no doubt have guessed I now plan to place Shêtân in stud, and before many months there will be a foal." He paused. "It will be yours, Alec, and I shall send it to you."

"Y . . . You mean, sir," Alec stared at him incredulously, "that it'll be mine? The first foal by the Black . . ."

Abu Já Kub ben Ishak smiled. "Yes, Alec, and out of Jôhar, the finest pure-blood Arabian in the world."

"Gosh!" Alec said dazedly, walking to the window. The view overlooked the valley, and in the late afternoon sun he could see the grazing horses. Apart from the others stood the Black, his head raised high as he surveyed his herd. He, Alec Ramsay, was to have the Black's first foal. His throat tightened at the thought. Perhaps it would be a colt . . . a son. The son of the Black! And it would be his, his alone . . . to raise, to take care of, and eventually to train for the track. What a horse he should be, with the Black for a sire and Jôhar for a dam! His eyes shining, he turned to Abu Já Kub ben Ishak and together they walked from the room.

ABOUT THE AUTHOR

Walter Farley's love for horses began when he was a small boy living in Syracuse, New York, and continued as he grew up in New York City, where his family moved. Unlike most city children, he was able to fulfill this love through an uncle who was a professional horseman. Young Walter spent much of his time with this uncle, learning about the different kinds of horse training and the people associated with each.

Walter Farley began to write his first book, *The Black Stallion,* while he was a student at Brooklyn's Erasmus Hall High School and Mercersburg Academy in Pennsylvania. He finished it and had it published while he was still an undergraduate at Columbia University.

The appearance of *The Black Stallion* brought such an enthusiastic response from young readers that Mr. Farley went on to write more stories about the Black, and about other horses as well. He now has twenty-five books to his credit, including his first dog story, *The Great Dane Thor,* and his story of America's greatest thoroughbred, *Man O' War.* His books have been enormously successful in this country, and have also been published in fourteen foreign countries.

When not traveling, Walter Farley and his wife, Rosemary, divide their time between a farm in Pennsylvania and a beach house in Florida.